A CAST OF CHARACTERS

AND OTHER STORIES

EDITED BY

SONNY BREWER

A CAST OF CHARACTERS

AND OTHER STORIES

EDITED BY

SONNY BREWER

MacAdam/Cage

MacAdam/Cage
155 Sansome Street
Suite 550
San Francisco, CA 94104
www.macadamcage.com

A cast of characters and other stories : stories from the Blue
Moon Café / edited by Sonny Brewer.
    p. cm.
  ISBN-13: 978-1-59692-193-1 (hardcover : alk. paper)
  ISBN-10: 1-59692-193-5 (hardcover : alk. paper)
  1. Short stories, American—Southern States. 2. Southern
States—Social life and customs—Fiction. I. Brewer, Sonny.
II. Title: Stories from the Blue Moon Café.
  PS551.C37 2006
  810.8'0975—dc22

                                              2006016114

"A Man" by Pia Z. Ehrhardt originally appeared in *Spork*. "Where Will
You Go When Your Skin Cannot Contain You?" by William Gay originally appeared in *Tin House*. "Your Body Is Changing" by Jack Pendarvis
originally appeared in part in *Nerve.com*. "Their Ancient, Glittering
Eyes" by Ron Rash originally appeared in *The Kenyon Review*.

Manufactured in the United States of America
10 9 8 7 6 5 4 3 2 1

Book and jacket design by Dorothy Carico Smith

THIS ONE IS FOR

DAVID POINDEXTER

Contents

A CAST OF CHARACTERS

AND OTHER STORIES

Introduction
by Sonny Brewer

AN OLD FRIEND OF MINE ONCE SAID TO ME, "You oughta go ahead and get the graveyard people to cut your stone now. Have 'em write on there, 'If this is anything like his life, he won't be here long.'"

I've thought a dozen times to get a paperweight-size version of that very epitaph. I'll get around to it someday. Or the graveyard people will.

Anyway, to this short attention span I'm blessed with, I sat at my breakfast table on an Alabama springtime morning, notions in my head sprouting like the green outside my window, spooning up some heart-healthy granola, and a thought ran by: What could we do differently with the *Blue Moon Café* anthology?

Nothing wrong with it the way it is. But that's not the point.

I thought about that little hardback I bought in the Pensacola airport, which fit so nicely into my sport coat pocket. I finished it before completing the loop down and back from the Miami International Book Fair, Gabriel García Marquèz's *Memories of My Melancholy Whores.* I fell so in love with that small volume that I used a couple of precious minutes of the allotted seven on my book fair panel to read from Marquèz's brief work that extends infinitely in my mind, its list of readers going on into another century, I am certain.

Aha! I smacked the table. Let's explore the axiomatic less-is-more philosophy and make the next *Blue Moon Café* book fit into a coat pocket, tuck neatly into a serious purse. Let's give readers a smaller portion, but more to digest. Let's spice things up with exceptional literary talent. More provocation. More beauty, horror, and sadness. More loving insight into the comedy and tragedy of our human situation.

And you, dear reader, will judge this effort. If you like this book, these fourteen writers—or most of them—then we will do it again just this way next year. Or, who knows, we've got notions aplenty, and miles to go before we sleep.

COPPERS: 1939
by Howard Bahr

HE FELT NO PAIN—THAT WAS GOOD, considering a dog was chewing his entrails. Good that it was dark, too; that way, he didn't have to see what was going on, though he could hear it—smack, smack, smack—and that was bad enough. Really, though, all he had to do now was rest his elbows on the drawbars and wait to die. If he hung on long enough, of course, it would start to hurt—the nerves would wake up, look around, realize what was happening, say *Whoa, man, we in some deep shit here!*—but he wasn't going to stick around for that. Before that happened, he would be dead. He was already drifting in and out, his soul pulling against the cord that bound it to life. Pretty soon the cord would break, and he would float off toward the stars, toward Orion and the Seven Sisters waiting overhead.

If he looked straight up, he could see plenty of stars in the open space between the tall black ends of the boxcars. That was funny, because a while ago it hadn't been any stars, just the low gray clouds and the mist. But he could see the stars now. They had moved in the time he had been here, shifting in the heavens, going on about their business. He didn't know many, but he knew the ones in Orion that his grandpappy had taught him, and he thought he would travel toward those when the time came. Now and then, when his soul went out into the dark, he could see the stars get bigger, brighter—could see that they were blue, not white, and could feel the heat from them. They were not cold, as he had always imagined. That was an important discovery, he thought, and he wished somebody was around to tell it to, but he was alone except for the dog.

Beyond the railroad yard was a screen of willows and cypress, a marsh, and beyond that the lights of houses, maybe his own house, though strangers would be in it now. The dog had come from somewhere over there—he hadn't got a good look at the animal but knew its kind well enough: a nigger dog, bony, shorthaired with a broad head and big muzzle, eat up with fleas, bare patches on his ass where he'd gnawed at himself. He had seen a thousand such dogs in his day and hated them all, worse than white people's dogs. Now this one had found some of his guts that were looping down under the couplers and chewed them loose and was eating them—he could hear it, even if he couldn't see or feel it.

"Go on, you son bitch," he said. "Be enjoyin' yourself, fuckhead dog." Then he forgot about the dog and found himself listening to the spring peepers in the marsh. That was a good sound. He heard whip-poorwills, and now and then an owl up in a cypress tree, and somewhere a mockerbird singing. A long time since he paid any attention to sounds like that. He could smell a sweetness—dewberry vines blooming in the yard, and privet on the edge of the marsh. That was funny, too—it was late December, almost Christmas, and who had ever smelled such things and heard such things in the deep wintertime?

Way off among the houses, voices and laughter, maybe a joint over there, people having fun. He wondered how much time had passed since the switch engine left the yard. The locomotive had steamed right past on the next track, lighting up the rails long before the engine passed. Switchmen were riding the footboards—he called out, but nobody heard over the noise, and pretty soon they were blowing for the crossings in town, and he was alone for a time until the dog came.

He closed his eyes and felt his soul drift out into the blackness; it was gone a long season, tugging at the cord. Or maybe it was just the dog pulling out some more of his guts. He supposed it didn't make much difference either way. In a little while, he opened his eyes again and saw the headlights of a motorcar on the road.

The Chevrolet belonged to the police department of the Southern Railway. The driver's window had been broken out one night last August, right under the noses of a half-dozen detectives on stakeout, prompting the Chief Special Agent to say that, all right, every swinging dick in the department could just freeze his ass off until the perpetrator was caught. Nobody looked very hard—in fact, no one looked at all—so now, in December, the detectives were freezing their asses off, even with the heater going full blast.

The wipers, clicking and clacking, smeared the mist on the windshield. The interior of the car was clammy and littered with brittle leaves of the autumn past, together with fusees, red and blue and white lanterns, a jug of coal oil, empty root beer bottles, yellowed sports pages from the *Times-Picayune* and *Meridian Star*—cheap novels, train manifests, and switch lists of freight and passenger cars long since dispatched into the dark of other nights. For weeks, a mildewed, round-faced doll had been propped in the back seat, smiling faintly, her glassy eyes gazing at her strange chauffeurs—or beyond them, or at nothing at all, just as the doll's little girl had been when they found her dead in an abandoned house by the right of way. Around the doll, like opened birthday presents, lay dozens of green .22 long-rifle boxes, some faded to the color of spring foliage, all discarded by Special Agent Hermann Schreiber, who burned up two boxes a night shooting any living thing in the lower orders of creation that showed itself on railroad property. Hido was engaged in an experiment to determine whether God could produce vermin faster than the Remington Arms Company could produce ammunition. So far, God was winning.

Tonight, as usual, Schreiber was behind the steering wheel. He loved to drive a motorcar, for it was always a novelty, always a challenge—and he always made the thing go too fast. Until he became an American, Schreiber had never driven a car or even sat in one much. In another life, he had been a gamekeeper on the forest preserve of a Bavarian nobleman, was thirty-eight years old when the army conscripted him for the Western front. He put his old skills to good use—French, British, Americans, who knew how many? God perhaps—until he was captured by murderous, wild-eyed United States Marines in the Bois de Belleau. Schreiber, who was scared shitless of the Marines, knew better than to tell them he was a sniper. In fact, he had never told anyone except his partner, Roy Jack Lucas, who had not been in the war, and who, right now, was slumped against the passenger door, rubbing his forehead as the car banged and jolted over the muddy track that ran along the south yard in Meridian, Mississippi.

Schreiber's delicate, almost toy-like double-barreled sporting rifle, wrapped in a poncho, lay in the back seat. Clipped upright to the dashboard was a Model 12 Winchester shotgun provided by the railroad company. Other items on the company inventory this night: the officers' switch keys, badges, handcuffs, blackjacks, the timetables in their coat pockets, the Chevrolet itself, and a .410 pistol under the front seat. The .410 had once been the property of a Jumpertown bootlegger, now deceased.

Schreiber carried a 9mm Luger pistol, a cheap

owl-head .22 throw-down, and a set of brass knuckles. He wore a gray wool overcoat, gray suit and vest, gray spats over black shoes, and a gray fedora. He carried three cigars, a Hamilton 992 pocket watch on the end of a gold chain, a folding wallet with twelve dollars, and a wrinkled photograph of his wife and two infant daughters who had died of influenza while Hermann was cooling his heels in a PW camp in Belgium.

Roy Jack Lucas wore a brown fedora, wire eyeglasses, a cheap raincoat, a brown tweed suit and vest, a Hamilton 992 pocket watch on the end of a gold chain, and, in a shoulder holster, his .38 caliber Smith & Wesson revolver. A pack of Half-and-Half cigarettes. Some matches from the Triangle Café. A Case clasp knife. A pint bottle of bootleg whiskey and an invitation to his son's wedding at St. Patrick's Church on St. Valentine's Day, which he did not attend. The back of the invitation's creamy cardstock was scribbled with notes regarding the theft of three hundred pounds of U.S. government cheese from reefer IC 5909 on a moonless night in November. The two detectives knew very well who had done the deed—a common thief, George "Sweet Willie Wine" Watson—but they were not about to tell anybody, for it would mean a federal rap and endless paperwork. Instead, they chose to be patient, hoping that one night Sweet Willie Wine would wander into the sights of Schreiber's Luger while committing a felony. Hido never missed. Never.

Roy Jack Lucas was sixty years old. At nineteen, he had been hired as a patrolman on the Mobile & Ohio. Before that, he could not remember much. He might if he thought about it, but he didn't think about it. Now he was a detective on the Southern. Had he been asked, he would have been hard-pressed to tell how such a thing had come to be. He had been married once, but he wasn't married now. He didn't remember much about that, either, except that his wife, Regina, had not spoken to him in the thirty years since their divorce; she would, in fact, cross the street when she saw him coming, even after all this time.

Roy Jack did not hate Regina in return. Years had passed since he had had the energy to hate anything except the way his partner drove. Hido knew only two speeds: all ahead and dead stop. "Jesus Christ," said Jack, cradling his head in both hands. "You missed a hole back yonder."

"Jackie, Jackie," said the other. "You ought to get your brain looked at. Hurting all the time, I think you got a tumor."

"Good," said Roy Jack, then had to put one hand out to catch himself when his partner stomped sudden on the brake.

"What the fuck?" Schreiber ground the gears, searching for reverse. "Did you see it?" The car lurched backward, then slewed back down the road, the transmission whining. When it stopped, Schreiber reached over and shone his flashlight across the main line. "My God," he said.

A man was shielding his eyes from the mist-swirled stab of the light. For an instant, Roy Jack thought the man was floating between the cars. Then he understood. He pushed open the door and stepped out into the mud. He had his own flashlight now, and saw the dog crouching, saw the black blood on his muzzle, saw what he was guarding between his paws. The dog looked up and snarled at him, his eyes flashing red in the torch beam.

"Be careful of the shit-eater," said Schreiber. He called all dogs shit-eaters.

"I will," said Lucas.

"Hold on, Jackie, I'll get him," said Schreiber, struggling to turn in the seat for his rifle. "Don't look him in the eye."

"I won't," said Roy Jack. He pulled himself onto

the raised ballast. The dog snarled again and stood up, bristling. Roy Jack drew the Smith and looked the dog in the eye and shot him six times.

"Well, shit," said Schreiber from the car. "You never give me a chance even."

Roy Jack stepped over the trembling body of the dog and put his flashlight on the man dangling in the couplers: a light-skinned Negro, perhaps forty, in an old barn coat and wool trousers and brogan shoes. The pants and shoes were soaked in blood and glistened wetly in the torch light. The man's face was lean and bristly, and he still wore his hat. The couplers had caught him just under his diaphragm, and his shoes were dangling an inch from the slag.

"Gahd *damn,* Cap'n," said the man, laughing. "You ain't fool around with no dog, does you."

Roy Jack had a ringing in his ears from all the shooting. He shook his head. "What?"

Schreiber was there, breathing hard. He looked at the dog, then at Roy Jack, then at the man. "What the fuck happen here?" he said.

The man shrugged. "I be crossin' through the cut, be stoppin' to light a weed. Now here I is."

"Shit," said Schreiber. He looked to the west where the yard was swallowed in darkness, no lights but the eerie red and green of switch targets, blurry in the mist. "They must've kicked in on the cut," he said.

"What?" said Roy Jack. His breath made a cloud, like the others', like the dog had made when it was still breathing.

Schreiber didn't reply. He went away, and in a moment returned with a blue lantern from the car. He knelt and lit the wick with a match, then handed it to Roy Jack. He did not look at the man in the couplers. "You go flag the head end. I'll get to a telephone. Jesus."

Roy Jack took the lantern and walked up the cut, past the black maws of boxcar doors, past a string of greasy black oil tanks and at last a half-dozen loaded gravel hoppers, their flanks silver with moisture. Now he realized what Schreiber meant. The cut wasn't coupled up when the switch engine shoved the hoppers down. The impact drove the two boxcars together just as the man was standing between them lighting his cigarette. Bad luck and stupidity. Niggers traveled up and down the yards all the time. The railroad was their path to town and back to home; it was where they picked dewberries in the spring; it was where they set out from when they left for Detroit or Chicago, huddled in an empty box or gondola, or underneath on the hog rods. Niggers knew about switching cars. They knew the rules as well as the railroad men themselves, and they knew what could happen if the rules were forgotten.

There were lots of rules: Don't stand in the middle of the rail. When you get off, face in the direction of movement. Always grab a long ladder. Don't wear rings—you could pull your finger off. Listen for the rollout. Watch out. Pay attention. Check the oil in your lantern. Never shine your lantern in someone's face. Always pass signals just like they are given to you. Don't put a placarded car or a car of poles next to the caboose. Don't leave a knuckle closed on the head end of a cut. Pay attention. You can't see a flatcar rolling at night. Don't put your foot in a switch frog. Turn the angle-cock easy. Make sure the engineer can see you. Stay in sight. Stay out from between cars. Don't couple air hoses in a cut that's not blue-flagged. Don't be afraid. Don't hesitate. Pay attention. Watch out. Watch out. Death is always there—in the slick grass, in the moment when you think of your girlfriend, in the great wheels turning—waiting for you to forget. So don't forget. Apparently, the nigger had forgot.

A brake cylinder was moaning air, and the cars

were groaning; Lucas paused long enough to set a hand brake so the cut wouldn't roll out on them. His ears were still ringing, but he could hear Schreiber grind the company car into reverse, then heard it whining backward down the road. Roy Jack hung the blue lantern on the first knuckle and started back again; he could see the car's headlights bobbing and blinking. He could hear the windshield wipers, click-clack. By the time he returned to the man, Schreiber had reached the lower crossing and was gone.

"I be breakin' the rules," said the man. "Ought not to been crossin' through, and them workin' up there. I know better'n that. Say, you ain't got a weed, has you? I can't get to mine right now."

Roy Jack shook out two cigarettes, lit them both, put one between the lips of the dangling man. "Smoking ain't good for you, what they say," said Roy Jack.

The man nodded. "I know *that's* right," he said. "Done killed me once already. Ain't it a bitch."

Roy Jack was reloading his revolver. "What's your name?" he asked around the cigarette. He slipped the pistol back in its holster, tight under his shoulder, under the tweed coat.

"Is you rai'road police?" said the man.

"Naw, we the goddamned Red Cross," said Roy Jack. "What you think?"

"Well, I think you might's well shoot me, too," said the man.

"Naw," said Roy Jack. "We'll get a amba-lance up here, fix you up."

"Huh—I know *that's* right," said the man, laughing. "What we gone do in the meantime? We could play catch."

"I ain't got a ball," said Roy Jack. "What's your name. I ain't seen you around here."

"Naw, Cap'n. I been off in Parchman ten years. They 'cuse me of killin a nigger with a screwdriver, but it wasn't me."

"I'm sure it wasn't," said Roy Jack, though he was sure it was.

Parchman prison farm was up north of Jackson in the strange, flat, lonesome Delta country. The man must have ridden down to Jackson on the IC, then over to Meridian on the A&V. Only God knew why he'd ended up in the Southern yard. It was no easy trick, that traveling, and it left a man filthy and exhausted and maybe a little insane. Roy Jack had rousted many a 'bo, and they were all crazy.

The man in the couplers waved his arm at the

sky. "Hey, you know them stars ain't cold, like you think they is."

Roy Jack did not have to look up to know there were no stars out, just the gray scudding clouds and the mist. "I didn't know that," he said.

While the man went on about the stars, Roy Jack took hold of the dog's hind legs and dragged the body across the cinders, laid it out between the rails of the main line. He would have thrown it into the water, but he lacked the energy, and anyway, it was coming apart on him. He stood a moment, smoking, and looked out into the marsh, at the black water and the cypress, all smelling of decay. The lights of Meridian, not many at this hour, made a dirty yellow stain on the clouds. Lucas could smell the dog's blood and the man's, and the bile soaking the man's trousers. He flicked the cigarette away. He looked at his watch, then took out his notebook and wrote down *12:01 A.M.* and *Cut in #1—negro male caught in couplers*—He turned and shone his light on the boxcar numbers, then wrote, *L&N 4139—B end—L&N 4250—A end.* "What's your name?" he asked.

The man groaned. Roy Jack tapped his pencil on the pad. "You'll get a stone from the county," he said. "They'll put a name on it or not, it's up to you."

"It's Watson, sah. Be June Watson. What you talkin' about a stone for, Cap'n? I ain't need no gahd-damn *stone*, man."

"Watson," said Roy Jack, and wrote it down. He moved closer to the man, trying to ignore the smell. "You any kin to Willie Wine?"

The man's eyes lit up. "Sweet Willie Wine!" he said. "He my baby brother! You know him, Cap'n?"

"Yeah," said Roy Jack. "Yeah, I know him."

He played the flashlight along the drawbars and couplers, then climbed the ladder and set the hand brake on the Bend car, just to be sure.

Beyond that, he could do nothing. His hands were greasy now, but he pressed them to his temples anyway, pressed hard until he saw lights behind his eyes.

"It sho' a small world, ain't it?" said the man. "Here I come all this way, see could I find him, first white police I come across be a friend of his."

"Look," said Roy Jack, "you in some deep shit here."

"Willie, he all right," said the man. "He done some bad things, know what I'm sayin', but he ain't no bad boy. He just need somebody—" The man stopped and drew in a deep, ragged breath. Roy Jack closed his eyes and waited. In a moment, the man said, "Whew! That was a long way."

"Aw, man," said Roy Jack, and put his hand against the sill of the car and vomited in the gravel.

"How come a mockerbird sing at night?" asked June Watson.

"'Cause he can, I guess," said Roy Jack, though he heard no mockingbird, not in the deep wintertime. He heard them often in the spring and summer when he couldn't sleep, their caroling loud down the quiet streets, a lonesome sound. Roy Jack looked down the road, hoping for headlights. He said, "How come your little brother is so no-account?"

"He ain't had a chance to be nothin' else," said June Watson.

"You believe that?"

"I believe I want another smoke," June Watson said. "I wants to get in all I can while I got time."

Roy Jack lit another cigarette and put it between Watson's lips. The man sucked at the smoke, and the red tip glowed and hissed. "Mmm," he said. "Half-and-Half. That's a premium weed."

Roy Jack said, "You'll have plenty of time to smoke."

The other laughed around the cigarette. "You

know better," he said. "Soon's they uncouple, I'm a dead son bitch."

Roy Jack knew that was so. He had seen two other men caught up like this. One was a switchman who hadn't paid attention; he had summoned his wife, spoken to her coolly, made her promise to get all she could from the railroad company. The other was a kid maybe fifteen years old. He cried the whole time and fainted when they opened the couplers. They never did get his name, and in seven years nobody had ever called to ask about him. Man and boy, they had lived only a few minutes after they hit the ballast. The sound of the lift lever was their death knell.

"You gone stay with me?" asked the man in the couplers.

"I'll be right here," the detective said.

"I want you to do it," said the man. "I want you to pull the pin."

"Aw, man," said Roy Jack. "I—"

"Nah, nah," said the man. "You the only one I knows. Needs to be somebody I knows."

"All right," said the detective.

"'Less you want to shoot me first," said the man. "I wouldn't mind that."

"I ain't going to shoot you," said the detective.

They were silent for a moment. The yard was like a cold slab of iron. Nothing was moving, and no sound but their breathing and the creaking of the cars. Finally, June Watson said, "You hear that mockerbird? I love to hear—"

"Shut up about that, goddammit," said Roy Jack. After a moment, he said, "Look here, you got any folks? Somebody you want us to send for?"

The man thought a moment. "Can you find Willie Wine?"

"Not 'less he wants to be, and if I do, I will put his ass in the can."

"Well, I know *that's* right," said the man. "He'll get the news tomorrow, I 'spect."

"I'll make sure he does," said Roy Jack, "one way or another." He would leave word at Wimpy's Café on lower Front Street, but the truth was, they probably knew already, the word going around in the juke joints and ramshackle houses of Jumpertown. Things came to them on the air, Roy Jack believed, like radio waves.

"I wisht I had a drink," said the man around his cigarette, squinting his eyes at the smoke. "A drink'd be a good thing 'long 'bout now. Steady my nerves."

Before he thought, Roy Jack had his bottle out.

Now he would have to let the nigger drink. Well, fuck it. He could wash the bottle. When the man had finished his cigarette and spat it out, Roy Jack reached up and put the bottle to his lips. The man drank, his Adam's apple bobbing up and down. "Take it all," said Roy Jack. He could smell the whiskey where it was dribbling out of the man's insides and mixing with the blood on his pants legs.

The man couldn't drink it all. He started coughing and spitting up blood, and Roy Jack took the bottle away. He wiped the neck on his shirt sleeve, then tipped it up and drank it dry in one long draught that burned all the way down. Then he flung the bottle into the marsh, heard it splash in the dark water. Roy Jack waited until the coughing was finished. He put his flashlight on June Watson's face. The man was grinning, his eyes crossed, the edges of his big white teeth rimmed with blood. "You awright," said the man. Then his face took on a puzzled look, and he lifted a pointing finger. Roy Jack felt a tingle in his spine and made himself turn around.

He thought at first it was an illusion of the uncertain light, a shifting of some vagrant shadow where the dark was rearranging itself. Then he lifted his light and saw that it was the dog. It was dragging its hind legs over the rail, slavering pink foam, the teeth bared and rimmed with blood like the man's. In the flashlight beam, its eyes gleamed red, and its breath was harsh and wet, coming in long gasps and plumes of mist. Roy Jack took out his pistol again and emptied it into the broad head. The shots were loud in the silence, echoing off the cars, but even at that, Roy Jack heard the rounds strike wetly and the skull crack. The dog jerked and trembled and died at last with its muzzle an inch from Roy Jack's shoe, and the black blood pooled outward over the gravel.

"Gahd *damn*," said June Watson.

Roy Jack's ears were ringing again. He stood with his pistol against his leg. Steam rose from the bloody rents in the dog as if it were smoldering deep inside like a slag pile. Down the main line, Roy Jack could see the headlight of the switch engine returning. Lights were turning into the road, too: a car, and another with a swirling red bubble. That would be Hido in the company car, and the ambulance from the nigger funeral home. A third car bumped over the crossing—the coroner, probably. It was unlikely they'd bring a doctor, not for this.

"It'll be okay," Roy Jack said. "It'll be jake in a minute."

"I know *that's* right," said June Watson. "It be getting' cold. You gone stay with me?"

"Huh?" said Roy Jack. Then, "Yeah, yeah. I'll be right here."

That was all right, then. Everything was jake, though the cold was settling in him. Pretty soon, a whirling red light was in his eyes, and he couldn't see a goddamn thing. Heard men crunching through the slag, heard their voices, but no words. After a while, words didn't mean anything anyhow. He tried to listen to what the white police was saying, but again it was no more words than the mockerbird singing.

The switch engine coupled so gently to the east end of the cut that he didn't feel so much as a nudge. The engine's headlight was dimmed, but still bright enough to hide the stars above him. That was all right, too—he'd be up there soon enough. He heard the mechanical clank and breathing of the engine, then he heard some words—"I'm gone give you some morphine, boy"—but he couldn't see the face of the man talking. He felt a little prick in his arm, and a warm feeling ran through his veins.

The white police had his hand on the lift lever and was looking at him. "Can you hear me, June?" he said.

"I can hear you," said June Watson. "Go ahead—pull it."

The police jiggled the lever, then turned his head, spoke to a switchman with a lantern. "I need some slack," he said. The switchman moved his lantern up and down, and the engine gave a little push. The couplers tightened, but it was still all right—no pain, just a squeezing—it felt pretty good, in fact, like an embrace, and June Watson drifted out a long way. When he returned, a mockerbird was perched on the drawbar, little gray and white fellow, flicking his tail, cocking his eye at June Watson. He smiled at the bird, then at the police man. "Go ahead," he said.

"Goodbye, June," said the white police.

"I'll see you over yonder," he said.

The policeman nodded. He turned to the switchman. "Back 'em up," he said, and lifted the lever.

Five and Riding Shotgun
by Stuart Bloodworth

SWEET WILLIAM MASHED HIS 4-F FOOT on the gas, piloting around our two-stoplight town a purple van, yellow flowers blooming on the doors.

On black shag carpeting, barefoot, my sister Susan sat Indian-style, long hair she pressed at night on the ironing board shrouding her face as she shuffled eight-tracks. I didn't know Sweet William would be brother-in-law, then ex, then folded away like a quilt, but I was five and riding shotgun, playing with the red-and-white feather hanging from the roach clip on the rearview mirror, watching houses and steeples whiz past tinted windows, my world without monkeys, helicopters, weird birds, and guns, all the stuff my brother wrote home about from the place I'd seen on TV, warm on the couch between Susan and her lover, watching soldiers carry bodies through tall grass.

A Cast of Characters
by Rick Bragg

I HUNTED FOR HER THE LAST TIME IN A HOT, wet, sticky gloom, mosquitoes needling the back of my neck. We had been blessed with blackberry winter well into May, cool and dry, but almost overnight the Alabama summer had smothered Bean Flat Mountain. The yellow pollen that had swirled on the springtime breeze now filmed the surface of the pond and caked the wet leather of my high-top work boots. As a boy, I had run barefoot and buck wild through pastures like this, chasing fireflies with a minnow net and a mayonnaise jar, unafraid of what hit in the waist-high grass. But now I armored my shins in leather, and I moved old-man slow and easy around the pond, listening for the rasp of belly scales on the dead stems of last year's weeds. The cottonmouths are surly things that will bite you out of simple meanness—no matter what the nitwit snake handlers on the nature channels say. Mature snakes have little to fear here in the Appalachian foothills except the big owls, the hawks, and, of course, her. She would come at them from below as they glided across the surface of the pond, open her maw to the size of a Quaker Oats container, and suck them in. Only the biggest bass take a grown snake that way, and she was as big—for her kind—as I have ever seen.

I raked at the mosquitoes with one sweaty hand, slid my index finger under the line of my spinning rig, and lofted a steel-gray rubber worm into a pond I could no longer see. Some people would have called it fishing, but fishing is a random thing—you fling a hook into space and wait for something dumb enough or hungry enough to bite. This was more specific than that. I hunted one fish, as I had for a year, going on two. I cast over and over well into the night, the mosquitoes humming in my ears, fluttering up my nose. I twitched the rod up to make the worm dance from the bottom, then cranked it in, slow, slower. Then again and again until…it seemed like someone was tightening a Crescent wrench onto the nerves between my shoulder blades.

She is bigger now, I thought, than the last time she was caught, when my big brother, Sam, the consummate patient fisherman, set the hook hard and watched a brand-new rod bend double under her weight. I remember the surprised look on his face as he tried to reel and wound up having to tap-dance along the rim of the pond, wearing her down. I remember how this man who has caught untold thousands of fish hooked his thumb inside her lip, hefted her, and caught his breath.

"Lord," he said, "what a fish."

I ran one finger down her green scales, a little boy again. Six pounds and more—from a stock pond.

The eye I looked into, as he showed her off, was as big as mine, cold and blank.

You have to read your own story into an eye like that, because it gives nothing away.

In it, I saw my own failure.

I have never caught a fish like that. In this place I was born, a place cut by rivers, drowned by massive man-made lakes, and dimpled by ponds, if you're not a fisherman, you're not much of a man.

But I could set it right if I could catch that one fish, that amazing fish. It didn't matter that she had already been caught. That only proved that she was real, not just another hopeful lie told over a creek-bank banquet of beans and weenies and saltine crackers.

You, I thought, staring at the yellow-scummed surface of the pond, are my redemption.

I remember that first time, how Sam had to reach his whole hand into your jaws to work loose the hook, how he reverently eased you back into the shallows, and even rocked you back and forth a little, like a baby, filling your gills. You scraped silt off the bottom with your thrashing tail and vanished. Sam then straightened the rubber worm on the hook and flicked it back into the water, and as soon as he took the slack out of the line, a smaller bass took it. As he cranked it in, the rod shattered into three pieces, and he stood for a minute, wondering.

"The big 'un ruint it," he said. The fiberglass had cracked like a spiderwebbed windshield, and then shattered, a moment later, when the little fish thumped it.

I learned to fish with a cane pole in baby-size hands, staring at the red-and-white plastic bobber. I graduated to a Zebco 202 closed-face reel by the time I was old enough to zip my own pants. On any given Saturday, my people caught enough crappie from the Coosa backwater to fill a washtub, and I can still see my Aunt Edna mixing cornmeal with diced green onion and commodity cheese, then dropping them into iron skillets for the best hushpuppies I have ever had.

Fishing was our birthright. My grandfather Charlie Bundrum, a folkloric figure, hunted for the giant catfish below the Guntersville dam with a massive snag hook screwed into the end of a pool cue. He simply stood on the rocks, waiting for the turbines to churn to life, bringing the big cats to the surface. And then he would swing the cue down, hard, and sink the barbs into the fish's head. There wasn't a lot of sport in it, maybe. But you could feed a lot of people with a fish as long as a loveseat. His boat was made from two car hoods welded together, and he never wet a line sober. But when he came from the river and took a nap, his wife, Ava, would find fish in his coat pockets. My own gentle Momma, with a cane pole and a snuff can full of cow manure and red wigglers, is a bream-catching machine.

There was not a bad fisherman in the whole damn bloodline, male or female, until me. I would cast beautifully into open water, but if there was a tree to snag up in, I would find it. And once I cast, I cranked too fast and jerked the rod tip too high, and made the fish work to catch the lure.

A patient man named Joe Romeo took me fishing for trout on the flats of Tampa Bay, and I caught a cormorant. You haven't lived until you've tried to remove a hook from a live bird. I don't drink much, hardly at all, but on a trip to Destin, Florida, as a young man, I got knee-walking drunk and waded out into the bay with a saltwater rig and a bowl of boiled shrimp. The Coast Guard was not amused.

Once, fishing a small lake with my brother, I hung my crankbait up on power lines that crossed the water.

"Just reel it up to about a foot shy of the line," Sam told me, "and flip it over."

I did as I was told and flipped too hard—and into the high branches of a live oak tree. Sam just stared.

"I do believe," he said, "that's the first time I ever seen that happen."

It is still up there, shining in the sun.

The path to my redemption—or what I hope will be so—can be traced back to the fall of 2002, when I used the money from a book contract to buy my mother forty acres of pasture and mountain land on the ridge where my grandfather, the expert fisherman Charlie Bundrum, had made whiskey seventy-five years before. Near the blacktop, just inside the cow pasture, is the pond, and the one fish.

It is a beautiful place, sandwiched between two

ridges of hardwoods, alive with deer and wild turkey and rumors of bears. The pond is shallow and clear on one end, where the bream form a moonscape of round beds in the spring of the year, and deep and green on the other, where the big bass hang suspended in the murk. A snapping turtle the size of a fourteen-inch tire lurks here, and I have my orders from Momma to shoot it if I can, because she is afraid it will eat her ducklings. There ain't much glory in shooting a turtle, so I hope it stays hid until one of us dies of natural causes. Her mature ducks dodge my casts, and her two miniature donkeys, just pets, come down to drink and snort. They have never seen a real donkey, and believe they are normal size.

The place is so green it looks painted on. The live oaks dip their limbs into the water, and the grass is waist high except where Sam has used the tractor to cut a trail for my mother to walk. The path blossomed with tiny yellow flowers. "Ever'where Momma walks is flowers," he said, and it struck me, for the thousandth time, how beautiful the language of my people can be.

It is paradise, this country, give or take a few billion ticks and red wasps and fire ants, but the pond is all I really see anymore.

I have fished it since the day we bought it, and, almost from that day, I have known she was here. It happened when my mother and I walked the rim of the pond, checking to see if her duck was on its nest. In the deep end, the fish floated.

"What is that?" Momma said.

"Bass," I said.

"It ain't," she said.

"Well," I said, "what is it?"

"Sea monster," she said, and walked to the house.

We got our first good look at her when she was on the bed. She had laid her eggs on the gravel bottom, then floated above, watching. I teased top-water baits across the very end of her nose and trickled worms past her lower lip—being careful not to drag the bait through the bed itself—and she either ignored them or followed them for a few feet before circling back to the bed.

I hooked her, I am sure, in the late spring.

I never really believed in the science of fishing—I always thought there was more luck in it than most people allowed—but I always paid attention when Sam lectured me on the mechanics. When a fish hits, he said, don't worry about popping the line in two or snatching the bait out of the fish's mouth.

"Break 'er jaw," he said. Set the hook hard and quick. Not only will it hold, but it will also keep the fish from taking that second gulp that will often pull the hook deeper into her guts.

When I felt the tug on the tip of the rod, I broke 'er jaw.

The fish—it had to be her—broke water, well and truly caught, but as I began to reel, I felt the line go slack and my stomach go sick.

It was her.

It had to be her.

I am forty-five years old. I guess I must face the fact that catching one fish would not truly cure me, would not alter my legacy as the worst fisherman in my bloodline. It is too late, I suppose. I would just be the bad fisherman who got lucky, once.

Still, as the dusk creeps over the ridgeline, I carry my rods and tackle to the edge of the pond. The day, another day, will end in disappointment.

But sometimes it also ends in fireflies.

A Man
by Pia Z. Ehrhardt

A MAN'S BEEN IN JAIL FOR SIX WEEKS awaiting trial. Lillian doesn't say his name. A man kidnapped her from the grocery store parking lot. He raped her at his house, and again in the desert, chopped her hand off with an ax and left her for dead in the brush, thinking she would bleed out, but high school senior Doss Williams, student union president, stopped his car and saved her life. He helped her into the front seat of his Mazda, found her hand in the scrub and wrapped it in his windbreaker, then raced Lillian to the emergency room. It was warm that day. While she waited for help on the side of the road, the wind blew sand in her face. When Doss saw her she was standing up, holding her arm over her head as if to slow the blood. Doss said he couldn't believe his eyes. He thought she was wearing a long sleeved red shirt but it was a white tank top. He was returning from the florist where he'd picked up his girlfriend's corsage for the senior prom.

Doss visited Lillian every day in the hospital. His girlfriend would come with him sometimes and sit in the chair and listen, but she just stared at Lillian, too afraid to say what was on her mind: *You are fucked up forever.* Lillian asked Doss to stop bringing her around.

The TV and newspaper wrote stories and took pictures showing Doss and Lillian together. He was 18 and she was 25, but they were treated like a celebrity couple in the small town in Arizona. At first Lillian would hide behind Doss so her bad arm couldn't be seen, but every day he built her confidence, made her not feel deformed and ruined. He watched them dress the wound, looked closely, amazed, at the way the skin began to grow over the opening and reseal. He brought checkers to the hospital and they played game after game. She pushed her checker with her stump, scratched her cheek, swatted at imaginary flies to make him laugh. In their most famous photograph, Lillian made an X with her arms over her chest so people could see what had happened. Good limb. Bad limb. Doss's idea. She hated their shock, and he said putting it out there would be the quickest way for them to get over it.

The doctors tried to reattach her right hand, but

the damage was profound, so Lillian was fitted for a prosthetic. She preferred the days when she had no hand, because it was harder for her family and her doctors to rush back to normal. When she put on the fake one it made her mother and father feel better and their faces relaxed. They were amazed, and imagined her recovery was a full-blown display of the human spirit, but it was theirs, not hers. They could get used to the idea of this if Lillian could pick up cups again and write.

While she learned to use the prosthetic, the physical therapist taught her to eat and wash and write with her left hand. She did well at these tasks. She was a model patient. Everyone stopped talking about the rape, the torture, and focused instead on the great success of her recovery, so grateful were they that she was at least alive. Winter came. Her parents returned to California and said they'd be back in the summer.

Lillian had a story, but the police wanted only the details, so she described the man—50s, thin gray hair, slight build and not much taller than she was, large hands with part of his ring finger missing—and answered questions about the inside of his house. The kitchen faced north, on the table there were unpacked grocery bags from Albertson's, a shorthaired mutt ran in and out of a small door and barked while the man raped her on the kitchen floor. His truck was white with thin red stripes down the sides. He didn't blindfold her, just kept a small, black gun pressed into her side.

They caught him at a motel in southern Colorado. He'd worked as a machine tender at the paper mill but had been laid off. They linked him to the murder of a woman, a student at the junior college, whose body had been found in the river the month before.

Doss brought Lillian barbecued chicken for lunch that day and they were watching the soaps like always, but a news bulletin came on and showed the man's arrest. He had on a red wool cap, but no coat. He shuffled in leg chains between two officers. They put him in the back of the police car but not before the man looked at the camera and smiled. Lillian began to shake. She asked Doss to turn the TV off. Doss said it was coming to an end and soon the man would go to trial and then prison and she would be safe.

The doctors had told her that morning that she'd be going home in a few days. Lillian didn't know how to thank Doss. A proper thank-you would also be a good-bye and she didn't want to let Doss go. His daily visits were like her morphine. She wanted to pull him in with her deeper.

Doss's cell phone buzzed in the pocket of his barn jacket. "I'm at the hospital," he said.

"Soon," he answered. "Can't it wait?"

He walked toward the window and looked out onto a parking lot. "The connection's bad," he said.

"Yeah, she's doin' okay." Snow started to fall behind him. "Tell your dad I'll pick up the venison." A gust of wind swirled flakes up instead of down.

"Love you, too," he said, softly.

The next day he brought smoothies for lunch and told Lillian he'd be out of town most of the spring. She wanted him to ask her more questions about the crime, anything. He didn't have to worry about going too far. He said, no, it was time to put this behind her, but she begged him not to do that. It wasn't behind her. It was on the sides of her, breathing next to her when she tried to sleep, inside her brain. He did ask. He sat beside her on the bed and held her bandaged stump in both hands and wanted to know: Was the blade of the ax sharp? Was the pain bad? How did she stand? Did she look at what he'd done? Doss looked embarrassed.

Lillian told him. The blade was sharp and the man brought it down only once. There was no pain at first and then she blacked out. When she woke, her arm was on fire, but panic and a strange energy lifted her on her feet. She wanted to go home. She didn't look at her arm, only down the road for the first sign of the first car that came over the hill—Doss's. She drew ugly pictures for him, crime scene postcards with her in the middle of them, so he would help her carry the terror not the memory, and be more than just her savior. She shocked him with details and made him her witness.

Doss sat quietly on the edge of the bed and listened. He said he'd kill the man if he had the chance. He wanted the man to get the electric chair and be gone from this world.

They listened to a Lucinda Williams CD Doss had brought. He knew Lillian liked her. Lillian closed her eyes and sang about how you can't put the rain back in the sky, moving her stump like a baton to the music.

Doss would go to college in the fall and marry his girlfriend and visit Lillian on holidays. His new wife would stay home because this friendship was just between them. He'd been her kind visitor and now he would leave her with her life.

There is still one part of the story she keeps to

herself because every night Doss prays for her, but she no longer believes. She told Doss more than the police know, but not the ending, not how during the rape the man sat up and began to weep, and screamed at the sky like someone was forcing him to do this. Lillian was praying silently for her life, but in that instant she felt pity for him, forgave him and told him she did, and that was when the man said, you're not fucking *God,* went to his truck, got the ax and cut off the hand she used to bless herself and the man.

The Safety Man
by Tom Franklin

AFTER HIS SECOND AFFAIR, when his second wife left him for the second time, Gary used the setback as a reason to start drinking. He found an ad in the classifieds and paid a twelve-dollar signup fee to become one of the millions of other assholes in therapy. But unlike the other members of his Victims of Abusive Spouses group, he felt ready to dive right back into the Singles Scene. The other members, all women, sobbed and choked in the church basement where they met each week. Sometimes they threw up. They said they needed time to *heal,* to *be alone.* Gary hit on them all.

He had a table-side lamp that cut on and off when you clapped your hands. Gary and a paralegal were underneath an afghan, struggling. When she slapped him, the light came on.

He got a breedless dog at one of those Adopt-A-Pet sidewalk fairs. It wanted to be walked all the time and ate the shit of other dogs—which Gary took as low self-esteem. Also, the dog barked almost exclusively at Oriental-Americans. Gary had a theory that a cruel Japanese or Chinese man (or a Korean) had abused the dog, but why should he, Gary, deal with someone else's fucked-up ex-pet? He had enough on his plate to deal with and eventually left the dog bungee-corded to a light pole in front of the animal shelter. He sat in his car down the street wearing a baseball cap, pretending to read a newspaper, until a chubby woman came out, looked around, and led the dog inside.

In the same week there was an incident at work, where he was the safety man at a large chemical plant. It made pesticides. Gary was in charge of seeing that no one got killed or hurt. He drove a yellow pickup with a clip-on siren and could often be seen updating the large poster in the plant cafeteria that said how many Safe Man Hours there had been. At present the figure was very high, 10,067.

The incident at his job was this: He showed up for work hungover and unshaven. One of his chief responsibilities was to make sure everyone's respirator fit tightly—in the case of a chemical leak, an alarm sounded and you fastened your mask onto your face. So it was of major concern that Gary's three-day-thick growth of beard might cause an imperfect seal on his gas mask. Imperfect seals were a pet peeve of Gary's, as everyone knew, including El Roy, the big black rent-a-cop, who refused to let the safety man on-site with his "fuzz."

Gary said Bug off, Shaft, and a shoving match ensued and El Roy had Gary in a headlock when a golf cart skidded to a stop and the plant manager, dressed in a tie and hard hat, tried to get to the bottom of things. First he sent the uniformed onlookers to their stations. Pesticides could not make themselves. Then he made El Roy let Gary up and call the medics to check out Gary's head injury.

It might be a concussion, somebody said. Look in his eyes. Get a flashlight.

I feel fine, Gary said, batting their hands away. A line of blood ran down his nose and he let it drip onto his white shirt.

Should we warm up the helicopter? asked the helicopter pilot.

No, the plant manager said. He stood and folded his arms. Take him in the Chrysler.

At the emergency room they sprayed the gash on his head and bandaged him up and gave him a prescription for orange pills that he later took with alcohol, though the label advised against it. When he called the plant manager's office, the plant manager's secretary told him he was to stay home for a week, without pay. He was officially reprimanded. A letter being drafted as they spoke. And in case he was wondering, the secretary herself had demoted the Safe Man Hours figure to zero.

He hung up.

In the lonely rooms of his rental unit, he realized how much he'd been relying on his job for stability. The way it gave him small, daily targets: Get up at six in the A.M. Turn on the coffeemaker. Clock in at the plant. Gas up his safety truck, take his clipboard off its nail, and start his rounds. Charge a twelve-pack at the Gas-n-Go on the way home.

Now where was he? Except for beer, the refrigerator was empty. His cable had been turned off because he'd forgotten to pay the bill, so he drank and watched the television snow until he noticed the flashing time on the VCR clock. At Abusive Spouses the women confronted him despite his bandaged head. They'd voted him out of the group.

You're an abus*er*, they said, not a *victim*. We've called your ex-wife—

Which one? he asked.

Get out, they said.

He fingered his gas mask and drank warm beer and took more pills sitting in his car underneath magnolia branches beside a cemetery full of strangers, then he got out and pissed between a husband-and-wife pair of graves. He looked at his wristwatch with a plan on his face. It would still be open. He would drive to the animal shelter and spring his fucking dog.

When he got there and double-parked, the clerk snapped her gum and told him someone else had claimed it.

That happened once in a while, she said.

No! Gary shouted. He suspected the dog was about to be euthanized, and strapping on the gas mask, he pushed his way through a flapping metal door and past the janitor in rubber boots and headphones. The room seemed foggy and every dog stood up barking. Cage to cage and no familiar shit-eating Oriental-American-hating dog of low self-esteem. Gary removed the gas mask and apologized to the janitor, who ignored him.

Maybe all life really was was suffering, and what counted most was how well you did at it. He walked back through the door and past the clerk dialing the cops. All the way home he drove fast and kept changing the radio. He remembered his first marriage, so many decent moments there. Like after they got cable. Man, there used to be some really good shows.

Where Will You Go When Your Skin Cannot Contain You?
by William Gay

THE JEEPSTER COULDN'T KEEP STILL. For forty-eight hours he'd been steady on the move and no place worked for long. He'd think of somewhere to be and go there and almost immediately suck the life from it, he could feel it charring around him. He felt he was on fire and running with upraised arms into a stiff cold wind, but instead of cooling him the wind just fanned the flames. His last so-called friend had faded on him and demanded to be left by the roadside with his thumb in the air.

The Jeepster drove westward into a sun that had gone down the sky so fast it left a fiery wake like a comet. Light pooled above the horizon like blood and red light hammered off the hood of the SUV he was driving. He put on his sunglasses. In the failing day the light was falling almost horizontally and the highway glittered like some virtual highway in a fairy tale or nightmare.

His so-called friend had faded because The Jeepster was armed and dangerous. He was armed and dangerous and running on adrenaline and fury and grief and honed to such a fine edge that alcohol and drugs no longer affected him. Nothing worked on him. He had a pocket full of money and a nine-millimeter automatic shoved into the waistband of his jeans and his T-shirt pulled down over it. He had his ticket punched for the graveyard or the penitentiary and one foot on the platform and the other foot on the train. He had everything he needed to get himself killed, to push the borders back and alter the very geography of reality itself.

On the outskirts of Ackerman's Field the neon of a Texaco station bled into the dusk like a virulent stain. Night was falling like some disease he was in the act of catching. At the pumps he filled the SUV up and watched the traffic accomplish itself in a kind of wonder. Everyone should have been frozen in whatever attitude they'd held when the hammer fell on Aimee and they should hold that attitude forever. He felt like a plague set upon the world to cauterize and cleanse it.

He went through the pneumatic door. He had his

Ray-Bans shoved onto the top of his shaven head and he was grinning his gap-toothed grin. Such patrons as were about regarded him warily. He looked like bad news. He looked like the letter edged in black, the telegram shoved under your door at three o'clock in the morning.

You seen that Coors man? The Jeepster asked the man at the register.

Seen what? the man asked. Somewhere behind them a cue stick tipped a ball and it went down the felt in a near-silent hush and a ball rattled into a pocket and spiraled down and then there was just silence.

The Jeepster laid money on the counter. I know all about that Coors man, he said. I know Escue was broke and he borrowed ten bucks off the Coors man for the gas to get to where Aimee was working. Where's he at?

The counterman made careful change. He don't run today, he said. Wednesday was the last day he's been here. And what if he did run, what if he was here? How could he know? He was just a guy doing Escue a favor. He didn't know.

He didn't know, he didn't know, The Jeepster said. You reckon that'll keep the dirt out of his face? I don't.

They regarded each other in silence. The Jeepster picked up his change and slid it into his pocket. He leaned toward the counterman until their faces were very close together. Could be you chipped in a few bucks yourself, he finally said.

Just so you know, the counterman said, I've got me a sawed-off here under the counter. And I got my hand right on the stock. You don't look just right to me. You look crazy. You look like you escaped from prison or the crazy house one.

I didn't escape, The Jeepster said. They let me out and was glad to see me go. They said I was too far gone, they couldn't do anything for me. They said I was a bad influence.

The Jeepster in Emile's living room. Emile was thinking this must be the end-times, the end of days. The rapture with graves bursting open and folk sailing skyward like superheroes. There was no precedent for this, The Jeepster was crying. His shaven head was bowed. His fingers were knotted at the base of his skull. A letter to each finger, LOVE and HATE inscribed there by some drunk or stoned tattooist in blurred jailhouse blue. The fingers were interlocked illegibly and so spelled nothing. The Jeepster's shoulders jerked with his sobbing, there was more news to read on his left arm: HEAVEN WON'T HAVE ME AND HELL'S AFRAID I'M TAKING OVER.

Emile himself had fallen on hard times. Once the scion of a prosperous farm family, now he could only look back on long-lost days that were bathed in an amber haze of nostalgia. He'd inherited all this and for a while there were wonders. Enormous John Deere cultivators and hay balers and tractors more dear than Rolls-Royces. For a while there was coke and crank and wild parties. Friends unnumbered and naked women rampant in their willingness to be sent so high you couldn't have tracked them on radar, sports cars that did not hold up so well against trees and bridge abutments.

Little by little Emile had sold things off for pennies on the dollar and day by day the money rolled through his veins and into his lungs, and the greasy coins trickled down his throat. The cattle were sold away or wandered off. Hogs starved and the strong ate the weak. It amazed him how easily a small fortune could be pissed away. Money don't go nowhere these days, Emile said when he was down to selling off stepladders and drop cords.

Finally he was down to rolling his own, becoming an entrepreneur, slaving over his meth lab like some crazed alchemist at his test tubes and brazier on the brink of some breakthrough that would cleanse the world of sanity forever.

The appalled ghost of Emile's mother haunted these rooms, hovered fretfully in the darker corners. Wringing her spectral hands over doilies beset with beer cans and spilled ashtrays. Rats tunneling in secret trespass through the upholstery. There were man-shaped indentations in the Sheetrocked walls, palimpsest cavities with outflung arms where miscreants had gone in drunken rage. JESUS IS THE UNSEEN LISTENER TO EVERY CONVERSATION, an embroidered sampler warned from the wall. There were those of Emile's customers who wanted it taken down or turned to the wall. Emile left it as it was. He needs an education, Emile would say. He needs to know what it's like out here in the world. There's no secrets here.

The Jeepster looked up. He took off his Ray-Bans and shook his head as if to clear it of whatever visions beset it. Reorder everything as you might shake a kaleidoscope into a different pattern.

You got to have something, he said.

I ain't got jack shit.

Pills or something. Dilaudid.

I ain't got jack shit. I'm out on bond, and I done

told you they're watchin this place. A sheriff's car parks right up there in them trees. Takin pictures. I seen some son of a bitch with a video camera. It's like bein a fuckin movie star. Man can't step outside to take a leak without windin up on videotape or asked for a autograph.

What happened?

I sent Qualls to Columbia after a bunch of medicine for my lab. He kept tryin to buy it all at the same drugstore. Like I specifically told him not to do. He'd get turned down and go on to the next drugstore. Druggists kept callin the law and callin the law. By the time they pulled him over it looked like a fuckin parade. Cops was fightin over who had priorities. He had the whole backseat and trunk full of Sudafed and shit. He rolled over on me and here they come with a search warrant. I'm out on bond.

I can't stand this.

I guess you'll have to, Emile said. Look, for what it's worth I'm sorry for you. And damn sorry for her. But I can't help you. Nobody can. You want to run time back and change the way things happened. But time won't run but one way.

I can't stand it. I keep seeing her face.

Well.

Maybe I'll go back out there to the funeral home and see her.

Maybe you ought to keep your crazy ass away from her daddy. You'll remember he's a cop.

I have to keep moving. I never felt like this. I never knew you could feel like this. I can't be still. It's like I can't stand it in my own skin.

Emile didn't say anything. He looked away. To the window where the night-mirrored glass turned back their images like sepia desperadoes in some old daguerreotype.

You still got that tow bar or did you sell it?

What?

I'm fixing to get that car. Aimee's car. Pull it off down by the river somewhere.

This is not makin a whole lot of sense to me.

They wouldn't let me in out there, they won't even let me in to see her body. I went and looked at her car. Her blood's all in the seat. On the windshield. It's all there is of her left in the world I can see or touch. I aim to have it.

Get away from me, Emile said.

Aimee had turned up at his place at eight o'clock in the morning. The Jeepster still slept, it took the horn's insistent blowing to bring him in the jeans he'd slept in out onto the porch and into a day where a soft summer rain fell.

Her battered green Plymouth idled in the yard. He stood on the porch a moment studying it. In the night a spider had strung a triangular web from the porch beam and in its ornate center a single drop of water clung gleaming like a stone a jeweler had set. The Jeepster went barefoot down the doorsteps into the muddy yard.

He was studying the car. Trying to get a count on the passengers. He couldn't tell until she cranked down the glass that it was just Aimee. He stood with his hands in his pockets listening to the rhythmic swish of the windshield wipers. The dragging stutter of a faulty wiper blade.

I need a favor, she said.

It had been a while and he just watched her face. She had always had a sly, secretive look that said, I'll bet you wish you had what I have, know what I know, could share the dreams that come for me alone when the day winds down and the light dims and it is finally quiet. She was still darkly pretty but there was something different about her. The grain of her skin, but especially the eyes. Something desperate hiding there in the dark shadows and trying to peer out. She already looked like somebody sliding off the face of the world.

I don't have a thing. I'm trying to get off that shit.

Really?

I've had the dry heaves and the shakes. Fever. Cramps and the shits. Is that real enough for you? Oh yeah, and hallucinations. I've had them. I may be having one now. I may be back in the house with baby monkeys running up and down the window curtains.

She made a dismissive gesture, a slight curling of her upper lip. Will you do me a favor or not?

Is Escue all out of favors?

I've left him, I'm not going back. He's crazy.

No shit. Did a light just go on somewhere?

He stays on that pipe and it's fucked him up or something. His head. You can't talk to him.

I wouldn't even attempt it.

I don't understand goddamn men. Live with them and they think they own you. Want to marry you. Eat you alive. Jimmy was older and he'd been around and I thought he wouldn't be so obsessive. Sleep with him a few times and it's the same thing over again. Men.

The Jeepster looked away. Blackbirds rose from

the field in a fury of wings and their pattern shifted and shifted again as if they sought some design they couldn't quite attain. He thought about Aimee and men. He knew she'd slept with at least one man for money. He knew it for a fact, The Jeepster himself had brokered the deal.

What you get for taking up with a son of a bitch old enough to be your daddy.

I see you're still the same. The hot-shit macho man. The man with the platinum balls. You'd die before you'd ask me to come back, wouldn't you?

You made your bed. Might as well spoon up and get comfortable.

Then I want to borrow a gun.

What for?

I'm afraid he'll be there tonight when I get off work. He said he was going to kill me and he will. He slapped me around some this morning. I just want him to see it. If he knows I've got it there in my purse he'll leave me alone.

I'm not loaning you a gun.

Leonard.

You'd shoot yourself. Or some old lady crossing the street. Is he following you?

He's broke, I don't think he's got the gas.

I hope he does turn up here and tries to slap me around some. I'll drop him where he stands and drag his sorry, woman-beating ass inside the house and call the law.

Loan me the pistol. You don't know how scared I am of him. You don't know what it's like.

The loop tape of some old blues song played in his head: *You don't know my, you don't know my, you don't know my mind.*

No. I'll pick you up from work. I'll be there early and check out the parking lot and if he's there I'll come in and tell you. You can call the cops. You still working at that Quik Mart?

Yes. But you won't come.

I'll be there.

Can I stay here tonight?

You come back you'll have to stay from Escue. I won't have him on the place. Somebody will die.

I'm done with him.

The Jeepster looked across the field. Water was standing in the low places and the broken sky lay there reflected. Rain crows called from tree to tree. A woven-wire fence drowning in honeysuckle went tripping toward the horizon where it vanished in mist like the palest of smoke.

Then you can stay all the nights there are, he said.

The murmur of conversation died. Folks in the General Café looked up when The Jeepster slid into a booth but when he stared defiantly around they went back to studying their plates and shoveling up their food. There was only the click of forks and knives, the quickstep rubber-soled waitresses sliding china across Formica.

He ordered chicken-fried steak and chunky mashed potatoes and string beans and jalapeño cornbread. He sliced himself a bite of steak and began to chew. Then he didn't know what to do with it. Panic seized him. The meat grew in his mouth, a gristly, glutinous mass that forced his jaws apart, distorted his face. He'd forgotten how to eat. He sat in wonder. The bite was supposed to go somewhere but he didn't know where. What came next, forgetting to breathe? Breathing out when he should be breathing in, expelling the oxygen and hanging onto the carbon dioxide until the little lights flickered dim and dimmer and died.

He leaned and spat the mess onto his plate and rose. Beneath his T-shirt the outlined gun was plainly visible. He looked about the room. Their switchblade eyes flickered away. He stood for an awkward moment surveying them as if he might address the room. Then he put too much money on the table and crossed the enormity of the tile floor and went out the door into the trembling dusk.

So here he was again, The Jeepster back at the same old stand. On his first attempt he'd almost made it to the chapel where she lay in state before a restraining hand fell on his shoulder, but this time they were prepared. Two uniformed deputies unfolded themselves from their chairs and approached him one on either side. They turned him gently, one with an arm about his shoulders.

Leonard, he said. It's time to go outside. Go on home now. You can't come in here.

The deputy was keeping his voice down but the father had been waiting for just this visitor. The father in his khakis rose up like some sentry posted to keep the living from crossing the border into the paler world beyond. A chair fell behind him. He had to be restrained by his brothers in arms, the sorriest and saddest of spectacles. His voice was a rusty croak. Crying accusations of ruin and defilement and loss. All true. He called curses down upon The Jeepster, proclaiming his utter worthlessness, asking, no, demanding, that God's lightning burn him incandescent in his very footsteps.

As if superstitious, or at any rate cautious, the cops released him and stepped one step away. One of them opened the door and held it. Doors were always opening, doors were always closing. The Jeepster went numbly through this opening into the hot volatile night and this door fell to behind him like a thunderclap.

In these latter days The Jeepster had discovered an affinity for the night side of human nature. Places where horrific events had happened drew him with a gently perverse gravity. These desecrated places of murder and suicide had the almost-nostalgic tug of his childhood home. The faces of the perpetrators looked vaguely familiar, like long-lost kin he could but barely remember. These were places where the things that had happened were so terrible that they had imprinted themselves onto an atmosphere that still trembled faintly with the unspeakable.

The rutted road wound down and down. Other roads branched off this one and others yet, like capillaries bleeding off civilization into the wilderness, and finally he was deep in the Harrikin.

Enormous trees rampant with summer greenery reared out of the night and loomed upon the windshield and slipstreamed away. All day the air had been hot and humid and to the west a storm was forming. Soundless lightning flickered the horizon to a fierce rose, then trembled and vanished. The headlights froze a deer at the height of its arc over a strand of barbed wire like a holographic deer imaged out of The Jeepster's mind or the free-floating ectoplasm of the night.

He parked before the dark bulk of a ruined farmhouse. Such windows as remained reflected the staccato lightning. Attendant outbuildings stood like hesitant, tree-shadowed familiars.

He got out. There was the sound of water running somewhere. Off in the darkness fireflies arced like sparks thrown off by the heat. He had a liter of vodka in one hand and a quart of orange juice in the other. He drank and then sat for a time on a crumbling stone wall and studied the house. He had a momentary thought for copperheads in the rocks but he figured whatever ran in his veins was deadlier than any venom and any snake that bit him would do so at its peril. He listened to the brook muttering to itself. Night birds called from the bowered darkness of summer trees. He drank again, and past the gleaming ellipse of the upraised bottle the sky bloomed with blood-red fire, and after a moment thunder rumbled like voices in a dream and a wind was at the trees.

He set aside the orange juice and went back to the SUV and took a flashlight from the glove box. Its beam showed him a fallen barn, wind-writhed trees, the stone springhouse. Beneath the springhouse a stream trilled away over tumbled rocks and vanished at the edge of the flashlight's beam. You had to stoop to enter the stone door, it was a door for gnomes or little folk. The interior had the profound stillness of a cathedral, the waiting silence of a church where you'd go to pray.

This was where they'd found the farmer after he'd turned the gun on himself. Why here? What had he thought about while he'd waited for the courage to eat the barrel of the shotgun? The Jeepster turned involuntarily and spat. There was a cold metallic taste of oil in his mouth.

Light slid around the walls. Leached plaster, water beading and dripping on the concrete, the air damp and fetid. A black-spotted salamander crouched on its delicate toy feet and watched him with eyes like bits of obsidian. Its leathery orange skin looked alien to this world.

Against the far wall stood a crypt-shaped stone

spring box adorned with curling moss like coarse, virid maidenhair. He trailed a hand in the icy water. In years long past, here was where they'd kept their jugged milk. Their butter. He'd have bet there was milk and butter cooling here the day it all went down. When the farmer walked in on his wife and brother in bed together. The Jeepster could see it. Overalls hung carefully on a bedpost. Worn gingham dress folded just so. Did he kill them then or watch a while? But The Jeepster knew, he was in the zone. He killed them then. And lastly himself, a story in itself.

When The Jeepster came back out, the storm was closer and the thunder constant and the leaves of the clashing trees ran like quicksilver. He drank from the vodka and climbed high steep steps to the farmhouse porch and crossed it and hesitated before the open front door. The wind stirred drifted leaves of winters past. The oblong darkness of the doorway seemed less an absence of light than a tangible object, a smooth glass rectangle so solid you could lay a hand on it. Yet he passed through it into the house. There was a floral scent of ancient funerals. The moving light showed him dangling sheaves of paper collapsed from the ceiling, wallpaper of dead, faded roses. A curled and petrified work shoe like a piece of proletarian sculpture.

The revenants had eased up now to show The Jeepster about. A spectral hand to the elbow, solicitously guiding him to the bedroom. Hinges grated metal on metal. A hand, pointing. There. Do you see? He nodded. The ruined bed, the hasty, tangled covers, the shot-riddled headboard. Turning him, the hand again pointing. There. Do you see? Yes, he said. The empty window opening on nothing save darkness. The Jeepster imagined the mad scramble over the sill and out the window, the naked man fleeing toward the hollow, pistoned legs pumping, buckshot shrieking after him like angry bees, feets don't fail me now.

The Jeepster clicked out the light. He thought of the bloodstained upholstery strewn with pebbled glass and it did not seem enough. Nothing seemed enough. He stood for a time in the darkness, gathering strength from these lost souls for what he had to do.

He lay in the backseat of the SUV and tried to sleep. Rain pounded on the roof, wind-whipped rain rendered the glass opaque and everything beyond these windows a matter of conjecture. The vodka slept on his chest like a stuffed bear from childhood.

It hadn't worked anyway; it might as well have been tap water. Things would not leave him alone; old unheeded voices plagued his ears. Brightly colored images tumbled through his mind. An enormous, stained-glass serpent had shattered inside him and was moving around blindly reassembling itself.

He'd concentrate on more pleasant times. His senior year in high school, he saw his leaping body turning in the air, the football impossibly caught as if by legerdemain; he heard the crowd calling his name. But a scant few years later he was seated alone in the empty stands with a bottle between his feet. A winter wind blew scraps of paper and turned paper cups against the frozen ground, and the lush green playing field had turned brittle and bare. He wondered if there was a connection between these two images and, further, what that connection might be.

A picture of himself and Aimee the first time, try to hold onto this one. Fooling around on her bed. Her giggling against his chest. A new urgency to her lips and tongue. Leonard, quit. Quit. Oh quit. Oh. Then he was inside her and her gasp was muffled by applause from the living room and her father chuckling at the Letterman show. Other nights, other beds. The Jeepster and Aimee shared a joint history, tangled and inseparable, like two trees that have grown together, a single trunk faulted at the heart.

Drink this, smoke this, take these. Hell, take his money, you won't even remember it in the morning. You'll never see him again. Ruin, defilement, loss. One pill makes you larger, one pill makes you small, one pill puts you on the road to Clifton with a Ford truck riding your bumper.

For here's what happened, or what happened on the surface, here's what imprinted itself on the very ether and went everywhere at once, the news the summer wind whispered in The Jeepster's sleeping ear.

The truck pulled up on Aimee past Centre. Escue blew the truck horn, pounded on the steering wheel. She rolled down the glass and gave him the finger. She sped up. He sped up. She could see his twisted face in the rearview mirror. The round O of his mouth seemed to be screaming soundlessly.

When she parked in the lot before the Quik Mart he pulled in beside her. He was out of the Ford before it quit rocking on its springs. He had a .357 magnum in his hand. As he ran around the hood of his truck she was trying to get out of her car on the passenger's side. Just as he shot out the driver's-side window the passenger door on the Plymouth flew open and she half-fell onto the pavement. She was on her back with her right elbow on the pavement and a hand to her forehead.

She looked as if she might be raking the hair out of her eyes. He shot her twice in the face. Somebody somewhere began to scream.

Hey. Hey goddamn it.

A man came running out of the Quik Mart with a pistol of his own. His feet went slap slap slap on the pavement. Escue turned and leveled the pistol and fired. The running man dropped to his palms and behind him the plate-glass window of the Quik Mart dissolved in a shimmering waterfall.

The man was on his hands and knees feeling about for his dropped weapon when Escue put the barrel of the revolver in his own mouth with the sight hard against his palate and pulled the trigger.

Now The Jeepster opened the door of the suv and climbed out into the rain. He raised his arms to the windy heavens. All about him turmoil and disorder. Rain came in torrents and the thunder cracked like gunfire and lightning walked among the vibratory trees. His shaven head gleamed like a rain-washed stone. He seemed to be conducting the storm with his upraised arms. He demanded the lightning take him but it would not.

Mouse-quiet and solemn, The Jeepster crossed the rich mauve carpet. Who knew what hour, the clock didn't exist that could measure times like these. This time there were no laws stationed to intercept him and he passed unimpeded into another chamber. Soft, indirect lighting fell on purple velvet curtains tied back with golden rope. He moved like an agent provocateur through the profoundest of silences.

This chamber was furnished with a steel gray casket, wherein an old man with a caved face and a great blade of a nose lay in state. Two middle-aged female mourners sat in folding chairs and watched The Jeepster's passage with fearful, tremulous eyes.

He parted another set of purple curtains. Here the room was empty save for a pale pink casket resting on a catafalque. He crossed the room and stood before it. Water dripped from his clothing onto the carpet. A fan whirred somewhere.

After a while he knew someone was standing behind him. He'd heard no footsteps but he turned to face an old man in worn, dusty black hunched in the back like a vulture, maroon tie at his throat. His thin hair was worn long on the side and combed over his bald pate. The Jeepster could smell his brilliantined hair, the talcum that paled his cheeks.

The Jeepster could tell the old man wanted to order him to leave but was afraid to. The old man didn't want to be here. He wanted to be ten thousand miles away, in some world so far away even the constellations were unknowable and the language some unintelligible gobbledygook no human ear could decipher. He wished he'd retired yesterday.

For The Jeepster looked bad. He was waterlogged and crazed and the pistol was outside his shirt now and his eyes were just the smoking black holes you'd burn in flesh with a red-hot poker.

He laid a hand on the pink metal casket. Above where the face might be. He thought he could detect a faint, humming vibration.

I can't see her, The Jeepster said.

The undertaker cleared his throat. It sounded loud after the utter silence. No, he said. She was injured severely in the face. It's a closed-casket service.

The Jeepster realized he was on the tilted edge of things, where the footing was bad and his grip tenuous at best. He felt the frayed mooring lines that held him part silently and tail away into the dark and he felt a sickening lurch in his very being. There are some places you can't come back from.

He took the pistol out of his waistband. No it's not, he said.

When the three deputies came they came down the embankment past the springhouse through the scrub brush, parting the undergrowth with their heavy, hand-cut snake-sticks, and they were the very embodiment of outrage, the bereft father at their fore goading them forward. Righteous anger tricked out in khaki and boots and Sam Browne belts like fate's Gestapo set upon him.

In parodic domesticity he was going up the steps to the abandoned farmhouse with an armful of wood to build a fire for morning coffee. He'd leaned the girl against the wall, where she took her ease with her ruined face turned to the dripping trees and the dark fall of her hair drawing off the morning light. The deputies crossed the stream and quickened their pace and came on.

The leaning girl, The Jeepster, the approaching law. These scenes had the sere, charred quality of images unspooling from ancient papyrus or the broken figures crazed on shards of stone pottery.

The Jeepster rose up before them like a wild man,

like a beast hounded to its lair. The father struck him in the face and a stick caught him at the base of the neck just above the shoulders and he went down the steps sprawled amid his spilled wood and struggled to his knees. A second blow drove him to his hands, and his palms seemed to be steadying the trembling of the earth itself.

He studied the ground beneath his spread hands. Ants moved among the grass stems like shadowy figures moving between the boles of trees and he saw with unimpeachable clarity that there were other worlds than this one. Worlds layered like the sections of an onion or the pages of a book. He thought he might ease into one of them and be gone, vanish like dew in a hot morning sun.

Then blood gathered on the tip of his nose and dripped and in this heightened reality he could watch the drop descend with infinitesimal slowness and when it finally struck the earth it rang like a hammer on an anvil. The ants tracked it away and abruptly he could see the connections between the worlds, strands of gossamer sheer and strong as silk.

There are events so terrible in this world their echoes roll world on distant world like ripples on water. Tug a thread and the entire tapestry alters.

Pound the walls in one world and in another a portrait falls and shatters.

Goddamn, Cleave, a voice said. Hold up a minute, I believe you're about to kill him.

When the father's voice came it came from somewhere far above The Jeepster, like the voice of some Old Testament god.

I would kill him if he was worth it but he ain't. A son of a bitch like this just goes through life tearin up stuff, and somebody else has always got to sweep up the glass. He don't know what it is to hurt, he might as well be blind and deaf. He don't feel things the way the rest of us does.

PUSH

by L. A. Hoffer

WHAT HAPPENS: When Arlene's uncle dies, she arranges the burial, locks the door to his bedroom, and lives as usual in his home, a tiny, wind-worn chalet built at a tipsy angle into the side of Beech Mountain. She takes the same morning walk as always through the back door and into the woods, sometimes carrying her longbow and arrows to test her aim on the old foam target; her uncle nailed it to a birch on top of the ridge when she was just seven, and she can't imagine taking it down. Burrs stick to her boots, and she will find pine needles caught in her braid throughout the day. Later, she drives to work—the eleven-to-eleven shift in the basement sandwich shop of Glen's General Mercantile. It is early November and the beginning of ski season; Arlene will hate this job again in another week when the underclassmen from Appalachian State will come in droves looking for six-packs, stomping their boots and tracking mud down every aisle, and when husbands from Asheville or High Point will buy up the bundles of overpriced firewood she chops behind the Mercantile each night after closing. All this for half-a-dozen slopes covered in man-made snow she hasn't even skied in some five years. And the money's hardly more than minimum wage, but Arlene has known Glen since she was in Ski Wee, and this job means she doesn't have to drive off the mountain to some other job in Boone or Banner Elk. Besides, since her uncle left her the house and a secret stash under the mattress, she isn't hurting.

On a Saturday when the wind blows hard as whitewater, a man with curly black hair and eyes the color of sassafras walks into Glen's five minutes before closing. He's come from the slopes and he's fallen frequently—snow coats his jeans up to the hip. He asks if he is too late for coffee; he asks if it would be too much trouble to get a cup to go. Arlene likes him. She likes anyone who comes in alone.

She hands him the Styrofoam cup. "Sugar's down the counter," she says, "How was the skiing?"

"Oh, that." He stares at the lid on the coffee and smiles. "I fell twice in the line. I chickened at the chair lift." He laughs at himself, and it is a laugh Arlene would have thought she could only hope for had she seriously thought of it before; it is downright inappropriate; it is a Roman Candle and Cap Gun laugh; it shakes her balance out of her ears; it makes her knees cave.

From the top of the staircase, Glen calls, "What's all that noise? You okay?"

Arlene slams the register drawer. "Just saying goodnight!"

The man is halfway out the door, waving, saying, "I might try again tomorrow."

And he does. He keeps skiing. He gets better, he tells Arlene.

It happens in the usual way: slow for a few weeks, then so fast she can't remember which day it was, all her thoughts thinned into dashes drawn so far forward in his direction. Before work, she braids her hair and considers this man—she now knows his name is Walsh—and where she might go with him after work. They drive, mostly—up Grandfather Mountain to the mile-high swinging bridge, to the Antique Barn in Banner Elk, to his crooked apartment in Asheville. They don't stay any one place for very long. Arlene loves him, she discovers, for that Backfire and Plane Crash laugh, for the way his longest curl sometimes sticks to his eyelashes, for his near-photographic memory and perfect recall for names and dates and books and films, for the way he takes care to remember the things that grate her nerves: 100% wool socks, mayonnaise on grilled cheese sandwiches, the slightest noise during sleep. They trade the usual stories: he tells her he had TB when he was nine; she mentions she used to compete in archery tournaments, a long, long time ago.

Arlene still hefts her longbow up the ridge in the mornings and tries not to admit how much of her Walsh does not actually exist, how much is a past and a future she plaits one detail after another—maybe he rock-climbed at summer camp, maybe he failed his first driver's test, maybe he will come over and unbraid her hair and soap her shoulders in the shower tonight, maybe they will go to Nag's Head for New Year's. She is trying to push to the moment he will become permanent. When she picks him up from Ski Beech after work, she takes the curves around the mountain a few miles faster each time.

What happens: On the night after Arlene's twenty-third birthday, the first natural snow of the season falls on Beech Mountain. There's a blackout and Glen's shuts down, and Arlene and Walsh circle the mountain in his Subaru with a gloved hand on each other's thigh, sauced with the slippery fun of it all—the snow, the sled in the trunk, the swish of the wheels on the road. Snow thickens on the road; the tires hydroplane and the car skids into a mailbox. Walsh puts the gearshift in reverse and folds his hands on top of the steering wheel. "Your turn," he says. It's the third mailbox they have toppled. Since they met, neither has been able to drive straight.

"It's your car. Your lousy driving," Arlene says, and Walsh opens the car door to the cold, follows his laughter into the falling snow, and balances the dented mailbox on top of the trash cans at the curb. That laugh—by now it makes her think of Paul Bunyan, Big Ben—won't stop.

Arlene yells, "At least make it face the street!"

Walsh sets the mailbox forward and gets back in the car. "I know a spot where even the postman doesn't go," Arlene says. She climbs into Walsh's lap. "I'll drive."

And they are off.

Two blacked-out miles down the backside of Beech Mountain, she pops the Subaru into four-wheel drive low and steers into the snow between two naked white birch trees, easing to a stop just before careening into the creek. They leave the car cranked with the heat gunning and the radio humming and squeeze into the back where Walsh unstraps the baby seat and pushes it into the trunk.

Walsh's wife—her name is Madeleine and the divorce won't be final for another seven months—has their daughter tonight. His wife used to drive this car; Arlene has never seen a photograph of her, but she imagines a woman entirely the opposite of herself, a tall woman with stylish, short blonde hair and a penchant for obscure rock music, behind the wheel a year ago tonight.

But Arlene pushes that thought away for later. She kicks off her pants, drops a knee on either side of Walsh's hips, and stares through the back windshield into the falling snow.

Maybe: Walsh's wife gave birth three months ago and hates the pregnancy pounds clinging to her hips; she hates that she hasn't smoked a cigarette or attended a concert in thirteen months; she hates that she has to wear an ugly, flesh-colored nursing bra with easy-access Velcro cups. In the mornings, Walsh wakes up with the baby at five. He works mostly at home on the computer—physics, velocity—and sends his data to a company that designs swifter airplanes. He brings the baby girl—her name is Mallory; perhaps she is named after his wife's grandmother—to the bed and lays her on her mother's belly. The sheets smell of cinnamon oatmeal, talcum powder, and dried milk. When Walsh bends to kiss his wife, she says, "Don't even try it, my breasts are killing me."

What happens: After the lunch rush at Glen's, Arlene hops in her uncle's old Volvo station wagon—he left her everything; Arlene's brother moved away years ago—and winds around the mountain to Alpine Ski Center where she whisks a pair of Rossignols (length 180) out of the trunk. Inside the shop, she finds Billy Greene alone as usual behind the counter—he's been working here for thirty years, has white hair and a tired mountain beard she's been telling him to shave since she was fourteen. When she slides the Rossignols on the counter, he fumbles the screwdriver in his hand, drops it on the floor, and says, "You can't be serious," because almost five years ago in January, Arlene wrapped her leg around a Frasier fir while hotdogging it off-slope and swore she'd never again set so much as a Moon Boot on Ski Beech.

"What are the odds," Arlene says, "that you can just give me a break, wax the rust off, and reset the bindings?"

Billy slides his finger down the edge of the ski. "No problem." As Arlene walks toward the door, he calls, "Wish I could be there to see you eat snow." Arlene gives him the finger as well as her most substantial grin. "Those were my uncle's skis," she says. "Treat them nice."

A push on the gas, a swing on the steering wheel—the drive back to Glen's is nothing to her; she thinks of everything but the road she knows so well.

What happens: Walsh brings Mallory to Glen's. She has skin the color of a pear and wispy hair that collects in a blonde mohawk. She wears a bulky red snowsuit and cannot really move except to wiggle her arms. Walsh stands her on the café counter, and Arlene gives her a finger to clutch, but she is really thinking *I am only twenty-three, I am only twenty-three.* For months after that day, she will consider what the saleswoman or the waiter assumes when they go out; Arlene learns to smile and say, "Oh, no, I'm not her mother."

Maybe: Walsh can't get used to fatherhood; he holds the baby like she has a detonator. He has been standing on tiptoe since that night over a year ago when his young wife—they had been married six months—stepped out of the bathroom in her underwear. He was twenty-nine years old, and he was thinking about sex; he was thinking about the tattoo of a feathery wing—his wife too loved flight— peeking out of the top of her panties when she held up the EPT stick. Madeleine just stared at the spot where Walsh sat on the edge of the bed in the dark and said, "We can be upset about this for five minutes. After that, we're going to be happy."

What happens: Walsh shows up at Glen's Mercantile with a season pass to Ski Beech. They hoist Arlene's skis—the fresh wax smells like pine needles—out of the storeroom and walk across the street to the slopes. The temperature steadies at twenty-eight degrees, and the snowblowers run at full tilt. Walsh holds her arm while she snaps into the bindings.

At the chair lift, Arlene holds her breath and grasps both poles in one hand and looks over her shoulder. These motions are still familiar—when the chair slaps the back of her knees and she sits, she exhales and looks at the lift operator in the booth, an unfamiliar woman with goggles thrust back on her stringy blonde hair. All the operators she used to know have moved off the mountain. Walsh lowers the safety bar and rests his arm on the back of the seat, cupping her shoulder. He says, "I like the way the chair swings."

"I wish they would speed it up," Arlene says. She is already thinking about how much better it will feel to cut the powder at the bottom. She is already thinking about how, maybe, in a few years, they will teach Mallory to ski on this slope.

New flakes big as teacups spill out of the snow-blowers below.

Maybe: Walsh sleeps with a strange woman whose eyes are more the color of maple sap than sassafras. He meets her at a bar, at a library, at a conference on physics. He says he married his wife too soon; he says he loves his wife. The woman unzips her plaid skirt, her green dress, her bootcut jeans. He drives home, pushes open the bedroom door, shoves his hand in his hair, and tells his wife. Weeks later, after she has moved across town with the baby, she calls him late one night and says she is thinking of pawning her wedding ring and spending the money on a new tattoo.

What happens: Arlene and Walsh hibernate at night. She begins to expect him regularly; he brings his laptop full of numbers and parabolas and graphs when he sleeps over; he shows her airplane simulations; he tells purposefully bad jokes—"I'm going to get on the computer, I hope I don't break it"—when he discovers it makes Arlene laugh harder than good jokes. They make and unmake the bed. Two nights a week, he picks up Mallory from his still-wife's house and keeps her overnight. If Mallory can't sleep, he buckles her into the baby seat and drives to Beech Mountain. She drifts off on the way, and Walsh carries her into the house where Arlene is waiting. Sometimes Mallory wakes up and crumples her ear like a tissue; sometimes she stays still as a hearthstone. She is now nine months old and crawling. One day, after Walsh brings Mallory by the store again, Glen gives Arlene a playpen that belonged to his children who are grown and long gone off the mountain. Arlene finally changes something; she moves her uncle's desk and books out of the loft and sets up the playpen, a trunk full of her old toys.

Sometimes, Walsh drives back to Asheville to compare data with another physicist, and he leaves Mallory with Arlene on Beech Mountain. The baby smells like a fortune cookie and is no longer shy; she likes to tug on Arlene's braid. She has delicate, thumb-shaped eyes the color of sassafras—same as Walsh—but Arlene does not tell him she thinks so, and she especially does not tell him she wishes she could find something of herself in Mallory, something much more than the tug on the end of her braid becoming so familiar, some imprint that might prove she too was here.

When Walsh returns, he bathes Mallory and rubs measured figure eights on her back until she falls asleep. He and Arlene eat a late dinner of chili or pea soup she has brought home from Glen's. They get in bed at midnight every night, and though he may only be talking about an airplane design, a hike he wants to take, or Mallory's new tooth, he whispers to her; it thrills her that he treats everything between them as a crucial secret. Sometimes, in the middle of the night, Walsh laughs in his sleep—that Heat Lightning and Hurricane Coming that wakens everyone.

What happens: On New Year's, there is another

snowfall. Ski Beech opens the only black-diamond slope—White Lightning—at twilight. Walsh is happy; he stands in line beside Arlene, knocking clumps of snow off his skis with his poles. On the chair lift, he cries, "To the top!" but the lift stops midway. They bob on the wire; they feel bad for the skier in the chair just in front of them, alone on New Year's; they look down and watch the blurry figures in goggles and puffy coats as they slalom below.

"What's taking so long?" Walsh says.

"Someone fell. Must be bad," she says.

The wait goes on for a while; the chair stops bobbing, and the snow falls more heavily, lit a dull amber by the lamps lining the lift. The snow coats their shoulders, whitens their hair. Arlene kisses Walsh to pass the time. Maybe fifteen minutes later, the lone skier in front of them bends over his lap and pushes himself off the edge of his seat. Legs tucked against his chest, he drops in a fold—and maybe it is the wind, or maybe it is just her eyes playing tricks on her, but it seems to take him some many moments to fall—and he only loosens the last second before landing. The man touches ground one foot just after the other; the only noise is light as a thumb-tap, a mitten-clap of skis on new snow. He turns around and sails, unharmed and soundless, downhill.

"That was twenty-five feet," Walsh says.

"That was something else," Arlene says, and she will remember this man—she will still sometimes hear the mitten-clap on fresh powder—at odd times: when she drops a scarf on the floor, when she pens a comma after the word *however,* when she pushes a *PULL* door by mistake. It is the only moment she wishes not to dash through.

Maybe: Walsh's ex-wife is happy in Asheville. She gets a new car, a new tattoo, a drummer to love who plays in a band called The Suitcase on the Airplane. She weans Mallory off breast milk, listens hard when the baby starts trying to speak. She takes the pill and leaves Mallory with a sitter sometimes if there's a good concert. Later, she recognizes the drummer isn't getting any more comfortable dating a single mother, and she finds a young dentist who is patient, who is used to waiting for bonding agents to dry.

What happens: Arlene and Walsh ski to the lip of White Lightning. With the delay on the chair lift, there are no skiers on the slope now, and the snow has already erased their trail. A wind at the top flattens their jackets. Walsh pushes off with his poles and bounces between the moguls, but the severe slant, the deep powder, and the Frasier firs thick at either edge cause Arlene to totter at the top, the tips of her skis over the edge. A third of the way down, Walsh cuts the snow waiting. He waves a gloved hand over his head, and she gives herself a push. It is smooth at first, though nowhere near as fast as she wishes she could slalom; she hunches low and spreads her poles above the moguls for balance, but there is a vicious ice just below the surface. Any minute now, the snow will stop; she will get stuck; he will take off his skis for her sake, and they will walk down.

What happens: Walsh moves in—there's room now, her uncle's books and camping equipment given to Lees McRae College—and Mallory sleeps over three nights a week. Arlene starts classes at UNC-Asheville, and Walsh stays home and works; at bedtime he reads about velocity until Mallory falls asleep. Always, Arlene remembers she is only twenty-three years old. One day, Walsh comes home and says that Mallory saw another woman with a long braid like Arlene's in the grocery store and said, "Arrrl." Mallory will start lifting her arms in Arlene's direction, even when Walsh is there to pick her up. He will stop getting up from his laptop to kiss Arlene when she comes home in the evening; his laugh will dwindle to a lowercase, to a mosquito buzz and a tire hiss. After a dozen other Fridays, Walsh will come home and push open the bedroom door and shove his hand in his hair and say he made a mistake, he is confused. It will only take him three days to pack, but he will leave things behind she finds every so often: a North Carolina trail map, a paper airplane, a crumpled ski pass. She will sell the house—it always was her uncle's house, she tells Glen—and move off the mountain. Some years later, of course, Arlene will be standing in line at a bookshop and look up to find a baby staring over her mother's shoulder with eyes just like Mallory's—like the imprint of two thumbs in the snow.

New York City Marathon
by Frank Turner Hollon

I'VE ALWAYS BEEN ABLE TO RUN. Some people are built to arm wrestle, and some are built to run. I'm a runner. Not necessarily fast, but steady, for long distances.

In my second year of law school at Tulane in New Orleans my buddies woke me up with a serious hangover at seven o'clock in the morning to run the Crescent City Classic. I ran ten kilometers (6.2 miles) in high-top tennis shoes without training. I've run the race every single year since then, but ten kilometers is not a marathon. I learned this the hard way.

It didn't seem like such a big leap from 6.2 miles to 26.2 miles. Simple mathematics, it seemed. Just run about four Crescent City Classics in a row. I was wrong. The marathon was designed with the purpose of truly testing the mental and physical strength of a human being. I probably learned more about myself training for and running the New York City

Marathon than any single event in my entire life. At the beginning of 1995 I sent in my registration fee and got all my papers together to run the race. I began to loosely follow a training schedule I saw in a magazine. Running a few evenings each week, four or five miles per outing, with a long run every Sunday. The schedule suggested increasing the long run slowly from six miles to twenty-two miles and then tapering downward a month before the marathon. I bought a sports watch and trained mostly alone.

I've always been a strong-willed man. Convinced my mind can overcome almost anything. I drank six shots of Jameson's Irish whiskey on my twentieth birthday in London because a drunk Englishman challenged my heritage. I refused to show any facial expression through the ordeal, and the alcohol had no effect on me. At least that's how I remember it.

During my training for the New York City Marathon I suffered from the ridiculous 1970s mis-conception that drinking water is a weakness. I didn't properly hydrate and saw no reason to waste time stopping for liquids. The adverse effects of this stupid notion will linger with me the rest of my life. I still get headaches each and every time I exercise vigorously, regardless of how much water I consume before, during, or after the exercise.

I never did reach twenty-two miles training on a Sunday. Instead, I usually got bored and stopped at seventeen or eighteen. During long-distance runs, the mind plays strange games. The body sends relentless messages of distress, and the mind slowly wears down until I would say to myself, "Nobody's watching. Just stop. Go inside. Seventeen miles is plenty. You'll be able to run twenty-six when you need to. Besides, maybe you lost count, maybe you've already run twenty. And even if you haven't, you can make up for it next week. Hey, what time does that football game start on television?"

Later, sitting on the couch watching the football game, I sometimes felt a twinge of guilt, but it wouldn't last long.

One time, on a hot Alabama Sunday afternoon, as I ran down a path alongside Mobile Bay, a fat kid came up behind me on his bicycle. I didn't hear him until he yelled loudly with the sole purpose of scaring the shit out of me. He was probably sixteen years old. I was thirty-one. He blew past me, and I sped up to a full sprint. The fat kid pulled away, flipping me the bird as he laughed.

The fat kid underestimated my endurance. Three

or four miles up the road I turned a corner to see him sitting on the grass next to his bike. He weighed about two-fifty. I weighed one hundred forty-three pounds, not counting my sports watch. Before he could get off the ground I was in his face.

With my nose actually touching his nose, and my right hand balled into a fist, I said with emphasis, "Say one word. Just say one single word, and I'm gonna beat the shit outta you right here. Do it. Say whatever word comes to your mind."

He didn't move. No sound came from him. He must have thought I was totally insane. A mentally ill jogger. We stayed that way a few seconds longer, nose to nose, before I stood upright and slowly jogged away.

I'm not sure why I added the part about the fat kid in this story. It's one of the few times in my life I've lost control. If he had spoken, I would've hit him, and maybe bloodied his lip. I surely would've been arrested and ended up in court trying to convince a judge I was justified in drawing my line in the sand between civility and chaos. The fat kid's dad probably would have waited for me on a Sunday afternoon around another corner.

Anyway, eventually the time arrived to go to New

York. The race date was November 12, 1995. It was cold and dreary. I woke up in my hotel room at five-thirty in the morning and took a taxi to a place in downtown Manhattan to catch a bus. There were thousands of runners gathered together and piling into buses parked back-to-back down the block. It was snowing lightly, and I was wearing only a short-sleeved T-shirt, red sweat pants over shorts, socks, and my trusted running shoes. It was instantly apparent I was underdressed and ill-prepared.

The other runners had jackets, hats, little sacks of accessories, and big green plastic garbage bags. For the life of me I couldn't figure out the purpose of those bags. Everyone was drinking from special bottles and eating energy snacks as the buses rolled toward the starting area at the Staten Island Bridge. The race was scheduled to begin at nine A.M., and we arrived at a giant open field on the other side of the bridge at seven o'clock to wait for the big moment.

The snow turned impolitely to rain. There were a few large tents already full of people. I learned the purpose of the big green garbage bags. People were inside their bags, safe from the rain, lying in the open field, huddled in groups mostly, with a few green mounds off by themselves. Women were lined up outside Port-O-Lets, and men stood urinating in the world's largest pee-trough. It stretched a full city block, with a river of urine flowing slowly downhill. I couldn't see where it emptied.

I stood at the pee-trough, looking left and then right, making sure not to glance at a foreign penis. I saw several women tired of waiting in their lines, squatting over the edge of the trough to relieve themselves. All the rules of society seemed abandoned.

I was freezing. I pulled my arms inside my T-shirt and tried to find a place in one of the big tents to sit down. A large percentage of the people who run the New York City Marathon each year are not Americans. Most of the conversations I heard were not in the English language. The only place available to sit was on the very edge of the tent, half in the drizzling rain and half under the tent. It was like a refugee camp. Body odors mixed with urine and the smells escaping from Port-O-Lets. There was a massive purge of fluids and solids from people as I nearly froze to death, eventually pulling my head inside the T-shirt along with my arms.

At 8:15 I heard the sound of a watch alarm, and then another, and another. I pushed my head through the hole in the T-shirt like a turtle to look around.

There was still a light drizzle. People began to emerge from their green bags. They stood, stretched, and drank more fluids. An Italian man, hairy and sleepy, stood beside me. In a single movement he pulled his sweat pants, shorts, and underwear to his knees, reached two fingers into a jar of Vaseline, and began to apply the jelly to the crack in his ass and elsewhere.

I stared a little too long at the Italian man, and he saw me watching. All around people began to apply ointments and salves. I saw several women lift their shirts and place Band-Aids on their chilly nipples. It was all strange and new, and I began to worry.

I drank some water and squeezed back in the pee-trough line. Runners began gathering according to their race numbers. The rain stopped, and the sun shined through, finally adding warmth. I hoped I wouldn't end up waiting at the starting line next to the Italian man with the jelly in his pants. I noticed that all the people congregating on the bridge were still wearing sweat suits, jackets, and sweatshirts.

Huddled together on that bridge, waiting for the gun to sound, people urinated where they stood, unable to leave their spots and go back to the Port-O-Lets or the pee-trough down at the field. I saw Kenyan runners, long and thin, warming up on the empty side of the bridge. They were stripped down to running shorts and shoes, their breath like smoke.

There were a few announcements. The runners set their watches. And then the gun sounded under a completely blue sky. Over twenty thousand runners moved forward en masse. It took me over four minutes to get to the actual starting line, and when the crowd thinned, I took off like a rabbit, darting in and out, over the bridge. There were piles of discarded clothing, sweatshirts, jackets, sweat pants. People undressed as they ran.

I covered the first two miles quickly. The humidity was low compared to Alabama, and the air was cool. I actually remember thinking to myself, "I've got an advantage on these Yankees. I've been training in the south. This is gonna be easier than I thought."

The streets were lined four or five deep with people cheering and whistling. It was like a Mardi Gras crowd. My adrenaline pumped as I passed by one water station, and then the next. I was running faster than usual. The crowd, the adrenaline, the blue sky, and my red sweat pants. I couldn't bring myself to throw away a perfectly good pair of red sweat pants.

We ran through Queens and Brooklyn, and through all the boroughs of New York City. I passed people eating energy bars and smiled at their silly rituals. I was barely sweating at all. Certainly nothing like those Sunday afternoons at home in the ninety-degree heat and hundred-percent humidity chasing fat kids on bicycles. I felt like I was kicking the ass of the New York City Marathon, and it felt good.

At about fifteen miles it didn't feel so good anymore. The crowd didn't seem to be as loud, and I noticed more and more people passing me. My knees began to ache. Training for the marathon, increasing my distances, weaknesses had revealed themselves. My physical weakness was my knees. The ankles and lungs never caused problems. Mentally, I had always felt strong. The first pain came from the knees, and as the pain grew, it worked on my mind.

At eighteen miles I reached a physical and mental place I had never been before. Running the early miles so quickly had taken a serious toll. Skipping the water stations and not drinking enough at the refugee camp left me dehydrated. Along with the pain in my knees, it was unpleasant.

It didn't become unbearable until mile twenty. I still had an entire Crescent City Classic left to run, and I could barely walk. It was the "wall." The place I had heard about. Where the body and mind cannot function or focus. A lady running in front of me lost control of her bowels and soiled the back of her yellow jogging shorts. The smell was nauseating. Thank God she was faster than me.

I stopped at a water station at mile twenty-one. I considered stopping for good. It was clear I hadn't trained enough. It was clear I had underestimated the monster. My nipples burned from three hours of rubbing on my shirt. My left nipple was bleeding a bit through the fabric.

There were jars of Vaseline on a table behind the cups of water. "What the hell am I doing?" I thought. "This is stupid. I've got a job. I don't know anybody in this city. I can just take a taxi back to the hotel. Sit in a hot bath. Watch a football game."

I stuck my hand in the Vaseline jar, shoved it down my pants, and felt the coolness on my raw skin. At mile twenty-three my mind came back to me. It seemed possible to finish. I could crawl three miles if necessary. Three miles was the distance from my apartment to the Marina. I could run those three miles inside my head. It could be done.

I trained with the goal of breaking four hours in

the New York City Marathon. At mile fifteen it seemed a certainty. At mile twenty-five it was an impossibility, but I didn't care anymore. I could no longer do math in my head. There was nowhere to put it. There was no room to think about anything other than taking the next step.

The crowd in Central Park was huge. Their enthusiasm drove me forward until I could see the finish line. The first place finisher had crossed the line two hours earlier. He was probably already home, having accepted his trophy, eaten lunch, and joked around with his fellow Kenyans.

I crossed the line in four hours, three minutes, and fourteen seconds. Once again, I was unprepared for what would happen next. The crowd of runners was herded forward, the sides of the roads were blocked so no one could sit down or veer off into the park. We were given blankets, and medals, and bananas, but always herded forward, with no end in sight. I fell down to my knees on the cement, ripping my sweat pants, blood rolling down my calves. I stood, pushed forward by those behind. We moved like a slow river for blocks and blocks to the center of Central Park where we were finally allowed to sepa-rate and spread in different directions.

I stood under the giant red "H" for Hollon, waiting for my father. Letters of the alphabet nailed on poles stood in a gigantic semicircle around the park, with people waiting for people under every letter. I sat down and started to cry. I just sat there, my face in my hands, and waited for my Dad to take me away. I waited for him to find me, and pick me up, and take me away, like I was a little kid.

The New York City Marathon literally brought me to my knees.

It wasn't until a month later that I began to plot my revenge. I registered for the 1996 New York City Marathon, sent in my papers, and began to train. I ran alone, twice during the week, with one long run every Sunday. I ran twenty-two miles three separate times, training mostly on a track. Round and round, mile after mile, with no crowds, and no distractions, like a mental ankle weight.

I drank water. I brought green trash bags and disposable clothes to New York. I put Band-Aids on my nipples and applied Vaseline where it belonged. I paced myself the early miles and smiled at the first-timers, wide-eyed and confident, passing me early in the race. I finished in three hours, fifty-six minutes, and forty-two seconds. No one had to lift me from the ground at the end. I finished strong, at full stride.

There are certain things a person should do in this life. Hold your baby in your arms, own a piece of land, jump out of an airplane, fall in love, get your heart broken, see the Grand Canyon, write a book, and run a marathon. Not just run a marathon, but finish strong, and leave with the feeling there's nothing in this world, nothing, that you can't do.

My Sestina, His Sestina
by Chip Livingston

The morning when my poem, a sestina titled "Coon Was Here," went online at *McSweeney's Internet Tendencies*, I got an e-mail from a reader in Dallas who asked about the poem's origin, specifically where I had gotten the idea for the piece, as his name was Jeff Coon, and the naming in the poem had struck a chord with his own history. I was startled. For one thing, I didn't know when the poem would be posted, and Jeff Coon's e-mail was my first alert that it was now available online; but there was also the coincidence to consider. My fictional character spoke intimately to a real person of the same name, who was a reader of poetry, of sestinas even (the only form of poetry that *McSweeney's* publishes is the sestina); he actually read the literary journal *McSweeney's*; and he happened to visit the *McSweeney's* Web site on that particular day.

I answered Jeff's e-mail and told him what I

knew of the story's origin: I identified with the sestina's protagonist, a mixed-blood Southeastern
Indian who was blond-haired and blue-eyed, and
who worried about not looking authentically
"Native." As a mixed-blood Muskogee Creek kid, I
hated looking nothing like what I thought "real
Indians" should look like, aside from not looking like
the other members of my family, and I vowed that as
soon as I was old enough, I would dye my hair black
to match that of my parents and my older sister. By
the time I was a teenager, my hair had naturally
turned a dark brown, but I still hated my blue eyes;
those I considered to be pointedly Anglo-Saxon. So
exploring these feelings about identity and appearance, along with perceptions of cultural expectations,
I came to imagine a fictional character named Ricky
in a similar position, who took his desire for darker
eyes to a further extreme, and I let his story be told in
what I imagined to be his younger sister's voice.

Jeff Coon in Dallas is also a mixed-blood Southeastern Indian, a Seminole whose grandfather was
given the surname Coon, based on his great-grandfa-
ther's Indian nickname, in order to sound more
"American" during a period of pervasive assimila-
tion. Jeff wrote me that he had never heard the name

Coon associated with any other Indians aside from his own family, and this had caused him to wonder how I came to write the sestina of my character's naming.

I'm thankful Jeff Coon followed his impulse to ask the question, which for me raised other issues, questions having more to do with audience than authenticity; about for whom writers are writing; and about the connections made between authors and readers on printed pages, on Web sites, and on audio systems around the world. It is a singular blessing for a writer to be made aware of these meetings, for the serendipity of such keen moments to be acknowledged, whatever the genre the writer is working in.

COON WAS HERE

I never called you Coon
though that was home Ricky
brother I still think is God
& pray to   bound by half our blood.
Mom's firstborn   by a non-Indian
you came out blond & blue-eyed.

I got my Daddy's Choctaw eyes.

& eyes are what made Poocha call you Coon.
Crazy bastard   with all your Indian
names. On your headstone it's Ricky.
But wolf is what you carried in your blood.
Poocha took it straight from God.

& whose eyes are bluer than God's?
Yet you put Mom's mascara to your eyes.
& burning them you tried to brown your blood.
Fisting them tattooed you like a ring-tailed coon.
From then on Poocha never called you Ricky.
But named you Coon, 'cause you were Indian.

Then named you again in secret   in Indian
& told you how your grandma bet the wolf his
    eyes
& won. I miss you so much Ricky
I swear to God.
I thought you were smarter than a damn raccoon
letting a bunch of rednecks make you doubt your
    blood.

By 17 you'd made spilling blood
a ceremony & finally learned to kick ass like an
    Indian.

You even hung a coon-
tail from your Pinto's rearview mirror. Eyes
still red from dope & daring God
behind your bangs. Then you did it Ricky.

You made the papers as a Richard.
But I want to write your name in blood
on the wall behind Geronimo's Spirits   where
    God
took you to rest with the Indians
through a western door where no one sees your
    eyes
& no one calls you Coon.

I'll write *Coon was here* & sign it Ricky
call you God & mix your blood
to paint forever closed your Indian eyes.

Holiday
by Thomas McGuane

I'VE WORKED FOR A PUBLIC UTILITY in the West for a quarter of a century and have had a good, I like to say honorable, career. But my wife, Carrie, and I are by no means rich and we are especially not rich by comparison with her sister, Teresa, and her husband Willi, a German sound engineer by origin and now a New York music producer, a naturalized American, and a man who does all his short term traveling—say, from the house in Connecticut to the office in New York—by helicopter. Teresa and Willi are "filthy" rich, and very nice people but they go so far out of their way to make the less well-off comfortable that the less well-off begin to feel in their presence like adored pets, a feeling whose assurances quickly give way to ambivalence or, in my case, ill-concealed anger, both of which are somehow unfair to Willi who has done all in his power to keep people from feeling ambivalent and angry, reducing their discomfort to wishing they had as much money as he, a harmless or at least unpreventable emotion.

So there, I have explained myself in a plain and unambiguous manner in the hope that henceforth anyone who hears my story will not be surprised by my behavior. If Willi would lose the strutting gait and lavish gestures he employs while showering benefits it might be that he would reap more genuine gratitude that he does at present. I work hard, I am fairly compensated, and I love my wife. She loves me and we are comfortable on our adequate acreage. By world standards we are at the top of the heap; but by the standards of Teresa and Willi we might as well be sharing an army blanket beneath an overpass. Carrie's loyalty to her sister and her arrangements are such that my discomfort at pet status annoys her and causes her to suspect at low moments that I am a disgruntled loser longing to be a music producer in a big limo, a big jet, or a big helicopter. At such times, she can go to hell too. From the beginning, it has been the vehicles that have created this discord. In my defense, I say that Willi and Teresa seem to lack the imagination to do more with their power than upgrade their transportation, at which point Carrie invariably nails me with some Puerto Rican Willi has sent to

Princeton, and I'm back to being an amiable house pet grateful for whatever kibble I can lay paws on. Still, I know that's not true. I know I'm impeccable. In my heart, I avoid toadying.

The utility I work for has a nice in-house health club and I, of all the functionaries serving life sentences there, use the gym more than any other, most especially the dumbbells. The result? I have a gorgeous body and really huge muscles which I feature in my selection of clothes. Willi has told me several times that he finds my big muscles tacky but I know on the animal level he realizes I could squash him like a bug. Once when he was drunk he said he thought big muscles on meek people—meaning me—were a joke. But I just love my body and may spend too much time in the mirror. Where I come from people want even their lowliest state employees to look like they could kick major butt. Plus, if Willi knew how I smoldered, he wouldn't call me meek.

Teresa was born with a pretty voice and a lively little acrobat's figure. Her days as a backup singer have paid like a slot machine. Her lavish availability as a pretty youngster appealed to an *occurrant* European like Willi; for everybody else, satisfying trysts involved little more than stopping by the house. That said, Teresa is a genuinely warm soul, a formerly generous person who has only lately taken on her husband's approach to getting on; and campaigns for appearances in the society pages she once despised with the asperity of an old hand. But, well, here I go again. Teresa is just as nice as her husband and I don't know what's the matter with me. I'll try to do better.

The inside of Willi's jet is paneled with exotic wood from the black forest, and feels like the sort of place in which huntsmen might put their meerschaums to good use. A banquette surrounds a black oak table that inverts to a broad screen where presentations can be made to folks seated there who are prepared to make far ranging decisions based on what they see on the screen. Today, we're headed to the Caribbean and it's frankly a marvel to watch the Atlantic unroll beneath us from the deep green of the New York shore, to the opaline of the Carolinas, the purple of the Gulf Stream, to the vaunted blue of the Antilles.

Willi reads his newspaper while Teresa sleeps and I watch the sea. Carrie is entirely focused on what the steward might bring us to eat, though we've been eating for hours. Carrie has tied a blazing blue silk ribbon around her shapely neck, which ought to please me but since she has never done this before I can only conclude that it is some kind of jetwear and it pisses me off. One or the other of the pilots periodically emerge to chat us up and show that they're just folk but Willi's cold glance soon has them scurrying back to the cockpit where they work. He uses a kind of dandruff flicking gesture for sending people away, so minimal as to appear to them as something they might have imagined. In their position, I would have flown us all into the sea. On the other hand, this approach to servants (including jet pilots) by Europeans wherein the status lines are never crossed seems to produce fewer misunderstandings than our American style in which the once-a-week housekeeper or boy who mows the lawn rebuke us for relationship failures or for having nicer golf clubs than theirs, or faster modems.

When my utility was deregulated, that is the company where I worked, a couple of things happened: rates went up for the cannon fodder, my retirement fund was imperiled, and a few of the executives got rich quick. I mention this because it is the first time private aircraft came into my world. I found that if you are well connected, though only for the moment, owners of private aircraft may give you a ride to where they are going. In this, private aircraft are different from private automobiles whose owners may take you where *you* are going. The few rides I got were to meetings where the kingpin needed actual knowledge to further his schemes, a thing I had and he had not. He brought the cavernous need and heart of darkness. I thought we were a hot combination but like a wolf, he fell to the spoils alone. In any case, I had a long drive in my car to get to the quick ride in the airplane and I felt I should park it well out of sight, laughable piece of shit that it is.

Our island villa looked out from elevated ground to an opaline bay. Milling servants and a wing floor plan limited the intrusions of guests upon hosts. Encountering Willi at the crossroads, his formality could be daunting and the illusion of the manse being really two houses connected by a broad emergency-use-only foyer grew palpable. I longed to ask him about the concentration camps but my beloved Carrie didn't seem to notice at all, a wedge. She ambled around the whole property and hung out with her sister on the sun porch, quickly learning the servants' names and even helping with their tasks in a consanguineous way that resulted in insincere interracial hugs. Teresa, on the other hand, treated them from a great height, having learned various vile new folkways from the German.

"Carrie and I can't thank you enough," said I, "Willi, this is some luxury."

"You're most welcome, Clem. Is there anything you need? Your rooms seem so far away."

Oh, right. Like you didn't get a floor plan from the rental agent. "It's all just perfect. We're able to come and go in marvelous comfort." I hate myself but not enough.

"I flat wish you all were a bit closer," said Willi. Of course I saw right through it. I particularly resent the suggestion that I would want to be any closer to him. In short, I embraced the floor plan. Keep your distance, thank you. Talking like a hillbilly is just another one of his obnoxious affectations.

The four of us went to lunch on the beach, at a little French place specializing in grilled fresh fish in the shade of tall palms and in sight of low aquamarine breakers too beautiful to be real and the former home of our lunch, bright snappers with their heads still attached, cooked over coals of native hardwood. It was simple fare, with the air of Caribbean living-off-the-land, $450, no VAT but exclusive of the gratuity produced under the glare of the chef-owner-waiter, i.e., a real toxic douche by displaced cheese-eating surrender monkeys. On the other hand, we were saving on heating oil. Willi picked up the tab but showed us the bill, occasioning Teresa to give Carrie a smile which I interpreted as, "Count your blessings, bottom feeders."

Teresa and Carrie went to the beach with a picnic basket of jerked pork leftovers, sliced mango, the short lived, single rising local bread, and a surprising amount of Danish beer. Willi watched them go down the walk to the palm shaded road, turned to me, and said, "The coast is clear."

"How do you mean?"

"I'm not sure," said Willi pensively. "Funny I should have said that." This is Willi being quote-unquote disarming. He has covered the bald spot on his head with a pair of Maui Jim wraparound sunglasses. He went on. "I suppose I was thinking that men are a strain for women, which makes it a strain on men. We hang over their lives like rain clouds. That's why they go skipping off like those two did: to be rid of us is to them just like the sun coming out after a dark day."

"I thought they liked us…"

"Believe me, it's highly qualified. We're a necessary evil. Not that they can't have a certain fondness for us but I assure you my friend, it is limited. They would far rather be with each other. When they're with their men, they're on the job. Some people like work but work is work, and we're work. Hence our two wives, two sisters, go skipping down the lane with a picnic basket. You take yours somewhere and see if she goes skipping down the lane. You're lucky if she doesn't look like she's being escorted to the gas chamber."

When Carrie and I go out to dinner it is true that she can make it seem like the Bataan Death March with a desolating T-bone or catch-of-the-day and Green Goddess on the iceberg lettuce at the far end.

"With each passing season I grow more childish in my rewards, and you rode down to the island in one of them. All week long I watch my clients file in, hats on backwards, pants falling down, clothespins in their noses, millionaires probably, if they can afford me. I put up with it, buy toys, and calculate how many people there are ahead of me on the escalator. Each year there are fewer. I take excellent care of my wife and consider myself idealistic for doing so while knowing that I'm just a walking-talking ATM machine. Days I think she kinda likes me, days I don't think she does but it's back to the drooling millionaires, one foot in front of the other."

"It's surprising you've reached of your profession with that attitude."

"My profession is greed. I don't know what you thought it was."

"My profession is keeping the good folks of the high plains warm in the winter."

"Well, bully for you. I keep crap on the airways."

"Maybe you should stop."

"And descend to your quality of life? Give me a break."

Well, to each his own. For a small town northern Protestant like yours truly, drabness is the outward sign of the sanctified. You can gauge who's going to heaven by how drab they are. Where I come from, we're all looking pretty good. If you don't think I'm going to heaven, you haven't been paying attention. People like me may slope toward heaven with our dreary sense of entitlement but we get to heaven nevertheless. Perhaps it makes us smug.

By the time Carrie got back to our room—the

wing!—I'd had a couple of naps and was teasing apart the pages of an old copy of *Time* that dampness and mildew had welded together. She sat down heavily on the bed and turned her sunburned face to me.

"Long day."

"Long day at the beach," I said and I admit the tone was corrective.

"I didn't realize how much time I spend just kind of going along with other people. Teresa never rests. She never lets anything go, ever."

"The whole New York thing."

"Not just the whole New York thing but the whole Idaho thing."

"I thought the whole Idaho thing was over."

"The whole Idaho thing is *never* over. The whole New York thing is a drop in the bucket compared to the whole Idaho thing."

"The little house on Prairie Avenue…"

"Exactly. She says we'll never really escape it."

"But she made you move to a better neighborhood."

"Not in time. She says our folks branded us as losers with that house."

"Whether they did or they didn't, they're dead."

"Clem, how could you! If you'd ever wintered in

the Prairie Avenue house you would choose your words with greater care."

"I wintered eighteen winters in a dump on South J," I shouted.

"Well, you're not chased into one psychiatrist's office after another by worn out linoleum like my poor little sister, you sonofabitch!"

I separated some *Time* pages and pretended absorption. I told her I was not going to get into this and cited the statute of limitations on parental inadequacy. My mother and father were perfectly nice and worked for the post office. I could hold it against them that I am a bureaucrat and public servant but I prefer to focus on all the little houses on the high plains I warm during many inclement days. It beats the heck out of recording dance tunes about robbing liquor stores or sponging off the working male in a MariMiko dress and black pearls. Okay, okay.

A beautiful young woman. I'll just leave it at that.

Willi asked me to go to the nude beach with him. What could I say? We drove the scooters across the island, stopping for croissants, and left our clothes draped over the handlebars like the others. This nude thing was no big deal because of the impact of Eurotrash on this tiny place. So many of the women bathers were topless that the only sexy ones were those who were fully dressed. What was disconcerting were the French male joggers, improperly secured, bounding along the surf line. We called it Propellor Bay. Willi had a reason for asking me to come here.

In our room after nightfall, I could see Carrie looking at me with concern. "I wish I knew why you were so uncomfortable."

"I have sunburn."

"You know what I mean."

"I feel tiny."

"Is that it?"

"And I don't understand this place. I went to the nude beach with Willi, and French businessmen were running in the sand with their dicks flying around. I don't get *that.* Willi wanted us to invite this person to dinner, Janet Gee—"

"—Janet Gee!"

"Yes, I—"

"Janet Gee the Broadway star?"

"I guess that's right—"

"What did she look like in real life?"

"She was naked." Unwittingly, I returned to the hick diction of my humble origins: "It seemed like

Willi might of used to know her or something. He was pressuring me to ask this stranger to dinner."

"Stranger to you and you only!"

"I guess you're right. People were semi mobbing her, you know, which she was eating it up. I'm the only fully dressed person there, not even a bathing suit, and Willi sends me out to invite Janet Gee to have lunch with us before we have to meet you and Teresa. He made it pretty clear it was going to be a covert operation. I had to kind of push through the crowd feeling real out of place. Miss Gee started walking away and I was hurrying to catch up with her glancing back and going faster and faster and people getting out of our way until finally she turned around and screams, *'Are you stalking me?'* 'Why no, I just wanted to ask you to dinner with our family.' *'You lie, you're stalking me!'* All those nudes started closing in and it was everything I could do to push my way out and get back to Willi. I was covered with sweat but Willi thought it was very entertaining. I suppose entertaining Willi is part of my job." Willi later described it as the highlight of the trip.

"Shall I have a word with him?"

"No but it was quite humiliating, Carrie."

"Don't look at me like that. I'm on your side."

I let this one go.

At dinner that night, we drank too much and grew more and more vociferous, to the point that the servants began hovering with that characteristically malignant glee they bring to the discovery that so much money makes people grotesque. I longed to jump up and tell them, in French I guess, "I'm average." But surely they'd never understand.

I first learned there was a problem when Teresa, fetching in an off the shoulder print dress of some "island" pattern, threw a double handful of well dressed arugula in Willi's face and shouted, "One word with Janet Gee and we speak through attorneys!" The little maid in her black and white uniform darted in to help clean Willi up. At first he resisted, then struck a regal or tragic pose while his face was wiped and the greenery removed from his chest.

"Well," Willi said, "that should do it for the hysteria—"

"—your title not mine—"

"—as I have had the ill luck to have employed the aforementioned as my secretary while she was still at Music and Arts and *well before* she became famous and incurred various rages—"

"Oh, honest to god, fuck you. Granted, I don't

think I could."

Carrie said, "I can't eat like this."

"So don't," barked Teresa. That was it. We headed for our wing, slabs of coral pink and sea blue concrete and a mean terrazzo floor and I was glad to go as these sister deals can get ugly fast. I could hear Willi calling out, "I love you" to us. We took the position that we were out of earshot. Some kind of palm scratched at the screen like a ghost and the lamps, all little more than waist high, cast a disquieting light across our torsos. At the end of the corridor a battle raged, and we could hear it, the clearest sound being a sort of tinkling which we attributed to all sorts of things but vowed not to go shoeless in those rooms.

"Teresa pretty much lost it," I said.

"Hardly. Willi's been on this Janet Gee for about ten years."

"Oh."

"That may be why we're here. How did you get into this, idiot?"

"He asked me to speak to her. It was a setup. She ripped into me and then spotted Willi. I think they enjoyed the trick. It was very awkward and several of the nudes looked like they might come out of the bag. I miss the mountains."

Carrie was applying face cream. For some reason she always crossed her arms over her face to rub her left temple with her right hand, her right temple with her left. I don't know why this aroused such affection in me.

When we were younger and never imagined a life in any place but Idaho, Carrie and I were fascinated by Teresa's generalized disgruntlement. She was persuaded that her parents lived in the wrong neighborhood—though they had lived their entire lives there—and blamed her father especially though his position as assistant principal of the middle school did not provide him a wide array of financial choices. Nevertheless, Teresa forced a move to a larger home that had just enough elevation to provide a river view, and that so taxed their finances that they unloaded it the minute she moved away but were unable to afford to move back to the neighborhood they left. Thereafter, they rented. Later, when Teresa married Willi and became rich, her then aging parents asked for help in moving back to the neighborhood where the girls had grown up. Teresa advised them to learn to stand on their own two legs, an odd suggestion to make to septuagenarians. That her mother was in a wheelchair made the irony obnoxious and Carrie started a fight with her that resulted in several years of silence, broken finally by the invitation to go on this trip.

Over time, we had come to think of Teresa as a force of nature. She was a well known figure now in New York society and on the board of the Westminster Dog Show—again one of those awful ironies: she had never allowed the family to own a dog. "I'll end up having to clean up after it." She even served in an advisory capacity to several music industry businesses, opportunities offered as a way of brownnosing her husband to which she never doubted her entitlement. In her set, she was a real tastemaker as to fashion and décor, requiring little assistance when answering the "What are you reading now?" queries from influential magazines, alternating thoughtfully between Dostoyevsky and Thomas Mann.

I acknowledge that I may hate Teresa. I think Carrie—if she were honest with herself—may find herself with stronger negative feelings about Teresa than she is willing to admit. I don't know and I may never know whether Janet Gee decided to have a little flutter with me to get at Teresa, get to Willi, or just joyride on my big muscles, a pleasure several at the utility have not denied themselves. When they do this, I lose all respect for them and their work situation goes downhill. So, you see I'm not such a nice person either but at least I don't lie to myself about it. But what happened with Janet and me had its good side, despite that I would get a good emotional thrashing over it.

Willi was under the casuarinas smoking a Gitanne. I guess he couldn't sleep either. Or maybe I sensed he was out there. When he saw me, he said, "There he is." It was a full moon. I was restless from the cognac we'd had at dinner and which always disturbs my sleep, on the rare times I have it. Carrie was in a little ball sleeping so sweetly. She gets it off her chest and goes to sleep. She could read the president the riot act and dream of baby lambs five minutes later. Willi blew the smoke toward the ground and watched it go. "You can just feel her hot blood, can't you?"

"Who?"

"Who! Janet Gee."

"She called me a stalker."

"That's what happens to animals like Janet: they get stalked."

While the moon was full, we had several of these

cigarette meetings. On one, Willi cast aspersion on islands altogether. He asked me if I had rock fever. Not in the first two days, I told him. If I'd been paying my own way, I'd have had fever of some kind or been seeking owner financing on the house salad which cost the same as the last snow tire I bought. Then he asked me to watch Teresa sleeping.

"Why would I want to watch Teresa sleeping?"

"I'd like to know if it's in the genes, the way she sleeps, with her head hanging off the bed for example and the pillow under her feet instead of her head and so on and so forth. To be determined."

"I can tell you now: Carrie sleeps very conventionally and very soundly."

"Indulge me, a quick glimpse."

We pushed through the bushes around the building, glossy green leaves with imbedded white flowers at the calyx, and no smell. I felt quite uncomfortable spying on Teresa asleep but once we were near the window, Willi gave me a shove and I found myself staring into Teresa's face, the hands clutching the bathrobe just under her chin. She wanted to know what I thought I was doing. I turned to draw Willi into view but he was nowhere in sight. In fact, I didn't see him until the next day.

I could have explained everything to Teresa and Carrie. Their looks indicated that they expected an explanation but I just returned them quizzically as though I couldn't imagine why they were staring at me. My failure to explain myself occasioned a good bit of self congratulation on my part. Was it a turning point? Despite my sense of having stepped into the unknown there was the unmistakable sentiment of new freedom. They could theorize all they wanted about what I was doing in that window but they'd get no help from me. I was blissfully unaware that I was being used by Willi.

Good civil servant that I am, I was still having some guilt at riding the jet to a faraway beach. Are my snowbound neighbors getting their electricity? My new egotism hinted that the utility would collapse in my absence, those proud and modest western homes darken into surprising night.

At a very awkward lunch at The Barracoon we had bowls of calaloo so dense with okra that it rose convexly from the bowls. We had grown accustomed to the savage and inconsiderate manner of the restaurant staff who made it plain we were lucky to be overcharged in their establishment. That the place would be decorated as an old slave market with shackles ringing the walls among pictures of celebrities who had dined there, I found distasteful.

The women went shopping down by the harbor and would later boast of having been flirted with by the crew of an English yacht, "a Swan 76." "Granted," said Teresa, "They had beautiful manners." Later Willi commented, "They learned the make of that boat by extensive conversation with the crew. It wouldn't surprise me if they had been aboard." Indeed, that night Teresa performed an aria of wishfulness as to life at sea, an aria fanned away by Willi as though it was a fly.

By now, Willi and I were seated congenially under a shade tree. I was enjoying a pleasant vacuity while mildly noting that Willi had something on his mind.

"About two months ago," he murmured, looking into the middle distance, "I began to be concerned with a persistent cough I'd had for several weeks. I decided to see my doctor." He paused for a very long time before continuing, then cast a significant glance my way. "My doctor said it was just a winter cough. There was no point in looking any further. 'Really?' I said. 'You're fired. Someone will call you for my records.' You simply must be proactive as all serious medicine is some form of triage with the best care going to the loudest and richest. You fight your way to the front of the line or you die. I have made significant contributions to Mass-General and pulled strings to see their throat specialist. I admit that I found him little more responsive than the quack I'd just fired. I pressed him hard. I gave him the feeling his back was to the wall. He ordered a battery of tests and we soon got to the bottom of things. Let's go for a walk."

We mingled at shop fronts with half naked tourists and admired the huge gems in one window. I was surprised there would be a market for this sort of thing on a small island and Willi assured me the gargantuan prices would not be offset by any tax exemption. "Even if you concealed them in your ass going through customs, you would be better off buying these rocks in New York." I couldn't take my eyes off the big sapphire. I'm such a rube! Plus, it was too big to go in my butt. Now that's a sapphire. But Willi said it was a fake.

Right at water's edge a small group was watching a man juggling swords. He had big hoop earrings covered with rust. "That's *so* Key West," said Willi. We paused at a kiosk where Willi examined a back issue of *Der Spiegel*. I finally had the nerve to ask about the test results. Without taking his eyes off the German paper wilting in the heat, Willi said, "It turned out to be just a minor cough." He beamed at me and said, "Gone now!" Willi can be so forceful that I nearly congratulated him on his recovery, but I didn't. The new me just looked at him without expression. I watched him try to figure it out. He must have wondered if I regretted his not being terminally ill.

"You know what, Clem? You should take some walks around the island, get a feel for the locals. I see what you think about this other stuff. Who knows, you might be right but I'm part of it and it's too late to change horses in midstream. Go down to the beach and look at the fishing smacks. Talk to the guys, the fishermen. That's the real deal. Not this. Not this, Clem. Go to the boats."

"I'll do it."

"I want you to go to the beach, see the boats."

"I promise."

"I'll make you a map. Five minute walk. Mornings are best. Net mending and so on and so forth. Get yourself down to those boats."

This is how my adventure with Janet Gee began: like the pigs at the Chicago stockyards that go up the ramps to their slaughter with a hook in their nose, I was heading to the fated shore. I had only one thought: "I'm supposed to be at work on Monday."

"Hey, stalker!"

It was Janet Gee.

The native fishing smacks were pulled nose to the shore and their crews were doing small repairs under a row of tall coconut palms. I'd been drawn here by the ring of a caulking iron as a muscular old black man drove a string of cotton batting into the seams of a red, green, white, and yellow smack. One boat with a stern anchor leading to a mooring buoy just off the beach had three young blacks in cutoff khaki shorts lounging beneath a net strung along the boom to dry. It was from this boat that Janet Gee had called to me.

"What brings you here, stalker?"

"The boats," I replied in my new flat tone. She was wearing what passed here for a modest bathing suit. It covered her nipples and her labia majora if she stood very straight. Such requisites of posture were difficult to attain and part of the planned allure had to do with when she would let her guard down, slump, or relax, throwing one or another attribute into view. Since I'd last seen her, she'd had her russet hair done in corn-rows and glass beads. She'd come a long way from Brooklyn's Music and Arts high school and it didn't look like she'd be going back anytime soon.

"Well, *this* is a boat. Why don't you come aboard?" She gestured to the handsome fellows and recited their names at which one after another they barely nodded. "Winston, Germaine, Terence." They got the same kind of nod from the new me.

The cockpit was filled with little paper birds and animals. "This is where I come to do my origami," she explained. "In another few days, these boys will be heading out to sea and there will be nowhere I can do my origami under open skies. I can't do it at my suite, of course, or anywhere on the island with all the fans. You've seen it, haven't you, stalker? Hardly room to breathe."

"I'm not a stalker," I stated feeling a little more dignified than when I allowed all my emotions to be heard in my speech. I don't think it's claiming too much if I say that it has helped restore the self respect appropriate to an official with an important public utility.

She grabbed my shoulder playfully. "I know you're not a stalker! Willi and I were just having a bit of fun. Isn't he a nasty little German?"

I had to smile at this, I'm afraid, more than smile really, just a big goober grin. Much tension went away. I even noticed objectively how really plain Janet Gee was at close range and when she wasn't projecting the star shimmer she had down pat, the cruel snapping green eyes, the cocked hip, et cetera. Janet got out a big sheet of paper and tried to teach me how to make a bird-of-paradise which ended up as a paper airplane. She laughed and threw her arms around my neck and the three fishermen smiled and made loose fists with their right hands which they raised and lowered in a gesture that meant self abuse to all the peoples of the world. I felt very awkward until a gust of wind caught the paper animals and whirling them around the cockpit, took Janet's attention elsewhere.

"I'm the only one Willi really loves."

"Oh?"

"Yeah, 'oh.' The only one. He could drop Miss Whosis off whatever cruise ship she wishes she was on and all he'd feel was that he was closer to me. He has actually sent me an e-mail telling me what she had and what I had better. It's an open and shut case. I'm in a precarious career and when it's over I'll be with Willi. You watch."

At first I thought she believed that I was opposed to what she was saying simply because of the blank look I had perfected. I felt I should show some interest or at least seem grateful for being so quietly taken into her confidence.

"I hardly think your career is precarious. Why Janet, you're a big star!" Precious little actual enthusiasm in my voice.

"I'm a big star on Broadway but Hollywood doesn't want me and soon Broadway will be dead except for *Cats* and if I haven't segued into Willi's arms, I'll be gone too." The little animals were whirling around the cockpit again and Winston said that the tradewinds were returning. The other two moistened and raised their forefingers, sarcastically testing the wind.

"It's funny that Teresa would have intuited all this, which she has."

"Intuit! She caught us. Willi could be in a world of hurt if it gets arbitrated."

What a terrible woman this is, I thought. I was swept by love for my wife and even new affection for Teresa by the simple expedient of contrasting them with Janet Gee. Everyone should have someone like her to remind themselves how lucky they are. The bits of clothing that hung off the lank frame of this predatorial actress seemed the most incredibly sardonic comment on the usual advertisements for procreation. I watched her look around sadly at all the twisted, folded paper in the cockpit. "Only the birds turned out. The butterfly, the crane, the eight pointed star, the strawberry, I fucked up. The whole elective thing at Music and Art gone haywire."

She bent to gather the paper. I wished she hadn't done that.

Carrie and I were in bed with the covers pulled up under our chins, shoulder to shoulder, a somewhat unpleasant sea breeze coming through the jalousies and the hostile vegetation of the tropics clawing at the screen. There was cotton stuck through a hole in each screen and without a doubt this meant that some halfwit native was warding off zombies. There were smoldering caracol bug repellents you could light as a last resort that not only kept the mosquitos out but made the room itself uninhabitable. Undoubtedly, the inventor of this annoying folly has a jet plane and nine homes. Nothing else is possible.

"It's a drag," said Carrie, "Teresa is thinking of leaving Willi."

"Why?" I know why it's a drag—no more perks—but I don't know why she's leaving, and of course, I know she's not leaving, because Willi is her good thing and she's not so dumb as to leave her good thing. Not while there's breath in Teresa's body, not while she's warm to the touch.

"Janet Gee."

I waited for a long time before I spoke. "Is there anything to this?"

"She keeps turning up in the same places they do. Where does she get the information? And then the fame thing must be tough for Teresa."

"I feel terrible for her," I intoned occasioning a measuring glance from Carrie.

"And," Carrie went on, "with you doing whatever-that-was in her window adds this whole other layer. What were you doing?"

I began to wonder what Willi had in mind putting me up to that, though he'd once given me his theory of "back-flushing" which had to do with circulating counter rumors and bad information when hostiles holding facts were closing in. It became plausible that by getting something between Teresa and me, a ridiculous idea, he could smokescreen his activities with Janet Gee. This may have subconsciously lay behind my decision to avoid defending myself, in that Teresa seemed to regard me increasingly less as a predator than as a nut. Now Carrie looked around the room as though seeing it for the first time.

"This is fun but it's so unreal. Maybe unreal is good. There's no reason for anyone to be here. Where we come from, everyone has to be there, don't they? I mean, they're stuck. On one of these islands, no one seems to be stuck. They're just sliding. Imagine living your whole life like that! I wonder if it's good being in a dream or if you get the whirlies. I think I'm getting the whirlies, Clem—" Carrie's tone began to darken. "—or worse, I think I'm losing it. I'd feel more normal if I were drunk. I went to that beach where Janet Gee was, people with nothing on but their jewelry. What if you walked down Main Street at home in just a necklace? Why is it so different here? I mean, aren't we all pretty similar? All us humans? What's happened here, Clem? Who are these people? In fact, who are Teresa and Willi? I don't feel so good. I want to take something for this, Clem. In another week I won't know who I am and I don't have any idea who you are if you're the one standing in Teresa's window with your God damn mouth hanging open."

I just smiled.

*

"There he is."

We were under the trees again, in the dark, smoking. Now I was smoking those terrible Gitannes like Willi and loving them. I'd look at a Lucky Strike and it was like, oh, no, I can't possible smoke one of those. Willi has really started opening up and I'm a smoker for the first time in my life. I never smoked in my school years or at any other time. It is so out of character for me to smoke that I feel reincarnated. The last few nights I've left the ciggy (that's how I now think of it) dangling from my lips in this kind of Belmondo thing, and wondering how much longer the smoke will bother my eyes.

"My father hates me."

"Your father is dead."

"Oh my friend, that is where you are so so wrong. They never die. They go somewhere else but they stay busy. My father was on a U-boat. I have a picture of him with his crew when they surrendered in England in 1945." Willi has no German accent, which I find only too German. "They looked like a bunch of kids and they sank a lot of nice ships. They were part of a worldwide epidemic of malice and all those men including my father—including Adolph Hitler who was childless!—are still here making the world the miserable place it is."

"At least you've got them dancing!"

"That remark ill suits you. You are usually a generous man."

"I supply heat to rural homes."

"You seem to have changed, Clem."

At this point our separate presences seemed to shrink to the two glowing cigarettes. I was aware of oppressing Willi and with thoughts of his many assets, his vast cheeseball, I began to feel a kind of underdog vigor. I wondered what he had done to deserve this and any sense of unfairness I might have had gave way to something pleasantly feral. I pictured him in a chalet as I turned off the heat, perhaps shutting down the whole resort and chair lifts. I never used to think like this. Of course it's impossible to use a public utility for personal revenge unless you're a member of Congress but that didn't stop my fantasies.

I had made several perfectly innocent visits to Janet Gee, frequent enough to recognize that her origami had improved: the lounging fishermen were different young fellows each time I went but every one of them had his own paper hummingbird. She had such a strong and honeyed presence that I soon lost my impression that she was scrawny and odd; by force of personality she had transformed herself in my eyes into something of a goddess. I'm not so much of a fool as to imagine she hadn't employed this talent on whoever crossed her path. But why she would lavish this on a little functionary from a state utility is beyond me, unless it's my body. I don't think I flatter myself when I say I caught her leering and I began to worry that I'd let her down, performance anxiety, et cetera. In some ways, she didn't have an easy life. She told me she sweated blood up there on the boards and in the end her mother was always trying to get her money. That's what those people call family values.

Willi announced a picnic. Do I think he really wanted to have a family picnic? No, he was just desperate to organize something and so a picnic it was, and a long hike on volcanic rock to a shining slot in the hillside that dropped to a blue sea, and me lugging the hamper down to the beach where the women were girls again with a very palpable jubilance that reminded me of my courting days when I had to take the two of them down the mud banks of the Snake River to slake the summer head in our humid, irrigated rural landscape where we swam in our underwear with averted eyes, years before Teresa moved to New York and by implication changed all of our lives. Until then, we had all looked forward to having children but now they were deemed too time consuming, and we were childless couples.

The fact that we are isolated in the separate wing of the house has given our vacation a strange quality. Our wing is in no way less luxurious than the wing of Willi and Teresa, but it has come to seem so. We feel our wing is on the wrong side of the tracks. But when we go to the beach it's strictly no-man's-land in terms of offsetting the feeling that we live in a bad neighborhood. This is what the poor get out of going to public beaches near the city. The girls liked this side of the island because it was one where the locals went and actually wore bathing suits, and what bathing suits! They reached from their Adam's apples to their knees. I felt somewhat risqué in the hot pink Speedo that does such nice things for my gluteus maximus. But I felt good about myself, especially when I ran my powerful body into the low surf like a locomotive. We had found a pleasant spot to ourselves.

At the sight of the breaking waves, Willi dropped

everything and rampaged down the beach, his stride slowed and broken only by the waves themselves until he upended in a cloud of foam. I've seen Germans do this before. Something gets into them. We watched him swim for a while until the current took him some yards down the beach and there we met him and let him tell us where to spread the tablecloth. I regarded in silence the splendid gesture with which he selected the shade of one of the two identical trees, the only trees near us, with the perfunctory air of one stating the obvious. I said I liked the other tree better—I mean, it was a joke—and I caught myself simpering apologetically. These are the sorts of things that make me glad that life is no longer than it is.

The sea made a narrow inlet into the volcanic rock and it would be necessary to cross it by swimming. I barely know how to swim and my eye catching physique is no help, muscle weight adding to the likelihood of sinking. The girls dog paddled to the other side, Willi backstroked, and I had no choice but to plunge in. I quickly found that it was a terrible error for I began to drown. Nothing could be more frightening. For someone as proud of his physicality as I am, scarcely moving a limb without care, to find oneself flailing and shouting and making foam is humiliation at its most acute.

While it lasts. Then comes real fear which is quieter. Followed by detachment which can result in noise resumption. I recall observing my extended lips outlined against a blue sky forming the words, "*I'm too young to die!*" as though they were the words of a complete stranger.

Willi fished me out, remarking only, "Jesus Christ, Clem," and letting it go at that. The girls made no comment about my narrow escape. It seemed plausible to me that this was the point at which I decided to repay Willi through Janet Gee. I had already caught her ogling my vibrant body and viewed that as a kind of family collateral. That it blew up in my face in no way undermines the original logic.

When I'd settled in to the warm sand next to my wife who held a paperback between herself and the hot sun, she said without looking at me, "You've been spending a lot of time at the boats."

It was the timing of this remark that chilled me to the bone: not two hours before, Janet and I had consummated our relationship in the hold of the native smack among bales of contraband cigarettes.

She'd ordered me onto my back and addressed me as "lunk" not "hunk," a disturbing nuance. I felt used and guilty, and it took very little to trigger my terror.

"A lot of time at the what?" I asked absently.

"Boats."

"There's something about that maritime culture that fascinates me."

"I think there's something about that Janet Gee culture that fascinates you."

"Is that the actress I showed my ignorance by not being aware of?"

"No, Clem, it's the bimbo with the paper birds you've been hosing."

I married Carrie a long time ago and began my career as a faceless functionary, seeking self esteem in home ownership and health club memberships which left me with the stupendous body, rippling abs, steel clenched gluteous maximus, a 24 inch neck that makes my head look tiny—bye bye thinking!— so unceremoniously mounted by Janet Gee, the Broadway star, occasioning a tiny squirt that threw my future to the wolves.

Then Willi hit it big and Teresa hit it big with him, soon letting him know what the charges would be if he strayed. She could always make herself clear and this ironclad contract became the basis of his deep respect for his wife as well as a marriage more or less as happy as any other. Willi sublimated what must have been substantially base urges into the more acceptable pursuit of money.

Carrie and I never really had that and I don't mean the money, I mean the contract. We've been auditioning from the beginning and I have just gotten the don't-call-us-we'll-call-you.

Here's how it played out. I don't want to change my whole life so I just took it like a man.

"How could you?"

"I really don't know."

"Would you like to tell me how it happened and what it was like? I might be able to handle this if it were less abstract, but no promises."

"You know when people try to explain how they lost control of their car? They say they overcorrected. It was like that."

"What I'm having the most trouble with is the expressionless way you're telling me all these things. Ever since we got here you've been like a robot. I wonder if Janet Gee found you robotic."

"Oh, I'm quite sure of that."

Normal compassion would, I was sure, bring a change of direction to Carrie's remarks. I was right: "Not only is what you did wrong between us but it is wrong for our family. I don't approve of Willi's interest and/or involvement with Miss Gee but you had no right to come between them. You might well have hurt Willi's feelings and he has been most generous to us. I can barely look my own sister in the eye because of what you have done."

"What about Willi in all this?" I asked.

"Oh, I get it. He sent you over to the boat."

"But isn't it so?"

"I love the inquiring look. You're good, Clem, you really are. Well, he and Teresa confronted their Janet issue and he came clean. Maybe you were meant to make her go away with your big muscles. Of course it's his fault but he has made amends while you have forced me to trap you like the miserable weasel you are." I know from past experience that once Carrie begins to express herself, however angrily, that there is hope. And when her fury abates and I have been forgiven, it will be seen that Janet Gee has added to my prestige, something I've been sadly lacking in our marriage.

If I can weather this—if I can avoid being forgiven!—my status will have greatly improved, not the same as being off the hook. I'll give up the weights. I'll shovel snow out to my car and take myself to work every morning. I'll be impeccable.

I explained all this to Teresa and Carrie on the ride home. The crew had brought Willi *The Journal* and he was lost in his seat up near the cockpit while the sea beneath us rewound the trip from azure to green to brown as Teeterboro, New Jersey grew ever nearer. Teresa said, "I don't know how you can call that closure. Granted, it provides you with the lowered hopes you seem better prepared to meet."

Carrie said, "Leave him alone, Teresa. He's had all he can handle."

I tried not to show my gratitude. I suppose we have a contract after all.

This was a good time to take a break and I went up forward to join Willi and his newspaper. I was going to ask him why he had betrayed me but the words never got out of my mouth. Without looking up from its pages, he said, "It had to be done."

"You might have ruined my life and my marriage."

"Cry me a river."

I said, "I don't think you're all that comfortable in

America."

"If you expect to ride in this jet again, you need to work on your dialogue."

By thinking of my muscles and of Janet Gee, I said, "Willi, if you keep this up, I'm going to force a landing."

"We're over water," said Willi wearily, going back to his newspaper. He seemed to detect something artificial about my rage for truth. He said I was out there.

Your Body Is Changing
(An Excerpt from Something Larger)
by Jack Pendarvis

Henry and his mother returned home from Wednesday-night prayer meeting to find an enormous owl eating sausage biscuits out of a torn sack on the kitchen counter. When they walked in the door it turned its head all the way around on its neck and looked over at them just as calm, and it was holding a biscuit in one set of talons like a man eating half a sandwich.

"Uncle Lipton!" hollered Henry's mom.

She went for the broom.

The owl knocked a whole slew of stuff off the counter as it craned and shook its broad wings. Henry's mom tried to tell Henry what to do, but he became confused and ran screaming down the hall.

The owl took off after him, emitting a constant stream of silky yellow defecation, but the short and narrow hallway did not accommodate its wingspan.

It lost control, destroyed a row of family photographs, and barreled into Henry's back. Henry fell on his chin, splitting about one inch of his tongue down the middle.

Henry rolled over to see the owl careen into the small, pale bathroom. It tore off the shower curtain and, wrapped and blinded, flew into the mirror on the medicine chest, smashing it into diamonds.

Henry scrambled up and shut the door.

"What have you done?" said Henry's mother.

"Now it can't get out," said Henry.

"But we *want* it to get out," said Henry's mother.

Henry spat a great bit of blood onto the floor.

They found Uncle Lipton curled up in a cabinet under the kitchen sink, next to the bug spray and Mr. Clean. His eyes wouldn't open all the way and he was humming a tune.

2

The chapel smelled like furniture polish. If Henry squinted, Amy Middleton from eleventh grade looked like Polly Finch from behind, the American hero who had been exploded in a methamphetamine lab as part of the war on terrorism.

The devil slapped a picture of Laura Prepon into Henry's head to get him off track so he couldn't concentrate on the word of the Lord.

Laura Prepon, the actress who portrayed the red-headed girl on *That '70s Show*, had gone on Conan O'Brien to talk about shooting a movie in Alabama. When she said Alabama, something happened in Henry's pants. Where in Alabama? Was she coming back? Why was the world keeping them apart? Oh, Laura Prepon, you have the wide, enticing face of a beauteous harlot. You have a vulva like a velvet boat.

It was eye-opening to be in Alabama. It was educational to find out that people could be so different, said Laura Prepon. One person from Alabama had tried to fashion a welcome sign for her as a gesture of goodwill, but this Alabama person did not go about his task properly. The sign was crudely constructed, which gave Laura Prepon a window into Alabama's soul, as she explained to Conan O'Brien. Alabama people did not know how to make neat, orderly signs, unlike the rest of the country. Another creepy person from Alabama actually tried to touch her in a coffee shop. Laura Prepon did not know how she managed to stay in Alabama for almost two weeks.

Henry wished he would see Laura Prepon

walking through a restaurant with everyone paying attention to her because she was a star of liberal Hollywood. Then he would stick out his foot real casual and trip her, not so she'd get hurt but just embarrassed, and everybody would laugh at her so she would know what it felt like. Then he would help her up and reassure her that people are people wherever you go. "For man looketh on the outward appearance, but the Lord looketh on the heart." Then he would insert his penis into her naked vagina and make a baby, her white legs wrapped all the way around him, legs just about as white as raw chicken legs.

But that was not the way he thought of Polly Finch. He wanted to hug Polly Finch respectfully and tell her everything was okay and lick the inside of her mouth with his tongue.

Poor Polly Finch! Minding her own business! And then she had spotted the innocent Chinese baby walking toward the methamphetamine lab in Upstate New York. Just when she tossed the baby out of the way into a soft bush everything blew up. Now she was paralyzed from the neck down and also from the neck up, but they thought she could understand what people were saying. One time somebody said something sad about Jesus and a tear had trickled out of her paralyzed eye! Another time the president had called her on the telephone and told her how it turned out those methamphetamine people had been sending money overseas for terrorism, and he thanked her on behalf of the United States for bringing everything out in the clear sunshine of truth, and while he was saying it one side of her paralyzed mouth went up in a smile. There were several witnesses! She was the Miracle Girl of Upstate New York and a warning to terrorists of all stripes that you can't get the American people down. There was that one home video where she was drinking punch in the weeks before the tragedy; they showed it on the news every night, and she stuck out her tongue and it was all red, bright red, as red as Kool-Aid! It was a famous image that had turned her into America's favorite paralyzed sweetheart and caused Henry to fall in love, even though she was nineteen years old and already out of high school and paralyzed all over.

Henry found that he was looking at the back of Amy Middleton's neck so much like Polly Finch's neck and the whitish hairs creeping up it, shaped like an arrow, darkening as they climbed, if you lifted up Polly Finch's long hair that smelled like apple shampoo to give her her special hospital bath you would see something like that underneath. Or if her beautiful hair was all bunched up in her special headgear that she wore for paralysis. He'd like to blow on the back of Amy Middleton's neck and watch the hairs waving like a pasture of tall grass. All at once his lips got so dry he could feel them cracking. One time Amy Middleton had walked by him after softball in her red shorts and he had caught a waft of something that smelled like a hot ironing board and made him dizzy.

The evangelist was saying:

"One evening at a state fair I came into my employer's luxurious trailer and found him crying his eyes out. Yes, this very same man with the world at his feet! I was stunned and flabbergasted. In my estimation at the time, he was infinitely my superior. I could not imagine why a person of such lofty attainments would ever need to shed a tear, and I told him as much, for we were as close as brothers in our way. This man gestured wearily between his wrenching sobs at his thousand-dollar monkey and his empty liquor bottles and the crumpled pornography that littered the filthy hole he called his home. 'Sam,' he said to me, 'all of this means nothing. I believe it is time for us to get right with the Lord.' And the name of that man was...Neil Sedaka. Who amongst you is familiar with Neil Sedaka?"

No one was familiar with Neil Sedaka.

"Calendar Girl?" said the evangelist. "Breaking Up Is Hard to Do?"

He was an old man with deep red wrinkles and blinding white needles of hair and nobody knew what he was talking about.

There was a time before the evangelist had been saved when he partook of mind-blowing drugs and toured with a band. They had "crashed" at a Catholic's house because there was nowhere else to stay. The evangelist had sprung awake in the dead of night with two searing pinholes of pain in his back. Well, it turned out there was a crucifix attached to the wall and the twisted face of the bloody tortured Christ was boring into the evangelist's back with little lasers coming out of his scrunched-up, pain-filled eyes. Only get this. It wasn't the drugs! The drugs had worn off. It was *real!*

That was an interesting story. It made Henry feel weird and excited, like when the man with the motorcycle had jumped over trash cans for the Lord or when the fat man had lain there with cinder blocks on his stomach and somebody had smashed them with a sledgehammer for the Lord, and the fat man got up and he was perfectly fine. That was in the gym.

The evangelist pointed out that the cross in the chapel was bare.

Real Christians worshipped the triumphant Christ no cross could hold, whose body was glorified, resurrected, and incorruptible, but Catholics had a perversion that bade them concentrate on fleshly things and worship graven images. They whipped themselves with whips and slept in coffins and all they cared about was the sick, dying human carcass that the Lord had discarded like the trash it was.

The evangelist said everybody should bring something to the fifty yard line to burn on Friday. Rosaries, crucifixes, pocket-sized idols of the Virgin Mary, whatever was Catholic you could get your hands on. One time he had burned some junk like that and you could hear the demons screaming as they spewed out of the fire, but he couldn't promise anything.

3

Henry Gill didn't sleep much. He was fourteen—a thin, worried boy with a wet-looking bowl of black hair and countless eruptions on his sweet, horrible face. He had big blue circles around his eyes, skin the color of skim milk, and a big soft lump on the left side of his chest.

They had thought at first it might be cancer but the doctors tested him out and discovered that his hormones had gone crazy. Henry had too much estrogen. It made the doctor laugh for some reason and then he stopped laughing and got serious.

"You are at a confusing age. I can assure you, however, that you are not going to grow a breast like a young lady. But please come back and see me if you do. Or seriously, if it gets any larger or becomes discolored or tender to the touch. My feeling is, it will eventually take care of itself."

But so far it hadn't.

Henry got free tuition to the Christian school because of his hardships. He lived with his mother and her uncle she had to take care of, an angry photographer who wore a bathrobe all day. Changes in photography trends and a series of near-fatal aneurysms had ruined Uncle Lipton's life and personality. He only came out of his room—it used to be the sewing room until he moved in—to drive his dying car to Hardee's for a sack of sausage biscuits and a dozen packs of mustard. It was all he would eat. He wouldn't drink anything.

4

It came out that before her tragedy Polly Finch had supposedly let some army boys take pictures of her showing her chest, also with her blue jeans unzipped and "touching herself." Also wearing a blue thong.

Henry hated the elite liberal media so much. They just had to ruin everything. Why didn't his pants realize the reports were unconfirmed? The devil kept popping pictures in his head of the twin pink bull's-eyes on Polly Finch's skinny chest, her shivering and shirtless, smiling at him, the chilly golden flesh of a nectarine.

He got out his book, the book his grandmother had given him, *Your Body Is Changing: A Christian Teen's Guide to Sexuality.* It was the greatest book ever. It smelled like cedar because he kept it at the bottom of his sock drawer. He wanted to understand his feelings.

Later that night Henry fell asleep on the couch watching TV. He was awakened when Jesus sat on the arm of the couch a little more heavily than necessary. Henry was surprised to learn that Jesus looked a lot like Luke, the scruffy diner owner on Henry's favorite television show, *The Gilmore Girls.*

"Hello, Henry, there's someone I'd like you to meet," said Jesus.

Henry looked in the doorway and saw a girl floating there, wearing a thin robe, bathed in orange light.

"Is that Polly Finch?" said Henry.

"Yes," said Jesus. "You sure are smart." And he rubbed Henry's head in a playful manner.

"Look, I've come out of my body," said Polly Finch. "I need you to put me back in."

"Okay," said Henry. "But I don't know how."

"Too late!" said Jesus. "You already said you'd do it."

Then in a twinkling Jesus was standing with Polly Finch, about a foot off the floor. He grabbed her hand and they flew away, presumably through the kitchen window. All this occurred the day before the owl got in and gave Uncle Lipton his famous aneurysm.

5

Uncle Lipton became a kind of celebrity within hours of being rolled into the emergency room. The X-rays showed a gigantic aneurysm, the biggest one yet for Uncle Lipton, maybe the biggest one ever for anybody. It was like a supposedly mild-mannered terrorist living in his head. Doctors the world over wanted to study him. There was this one doctor in London, England, who said come on over, the ticket's on me! There wasn't a moment to lose.

Everybody said this was the man to see. If he couldn't fix Uncle Lipton nobody could.

One doctor told Henry not to eat solids for awhile and gave him some gel for his tongue, which he had injured during the fracas with the owl. The gel turned Henry's whole head numb and cozy. All of a sudden he was on a helicopter pad on top of the hospital and his mother was telling him goodbye.

"Are you sure you're going to be okay while I'm gone to London, England?"

"Yes, ma'am."

"Call Ruth Ann, okay? She'll take care of you. Tell her I'm sorry this is so sudden."

A scientist pointed at his watch.

Henry's mother got into the helicopter with Uncle Lipton. The blades sliced the sky, faster and faster, and everyone had to go back inside the hospital. Henry's mother told him something, but he couldn't hear what.

6

Henry called animal control from a pay phone in the lobby and told them, "I got a sick owl in my house."

After that, he took off walking. He walked through the glass doors and the vestibule and another set of glass doors and across the wide parking lot into the decorative trees and he just kept walking.

November in Alabama had been until that point as hot as a furnace, but the Lord saw fit to put a tribulation in Henry's path. The Lord found Henry in nothing but his good blue pants and a white T-shirt spotted with blood from his broken tongue and his hard black school shoes with no socks (Henry must have left the socks, along with his church shirt, in the scooped seat of the doctor's plastic chair), and He blew a cold front through the state with whipping winds.

Henry was in a wild wooded area, to which the hospital's landscaping had subtly given way, when he remembered a video about devil worshippers they had watched in social studies class. A repentant devil worshipper with long sideburns had explained that when you first try to sell your soul to the devil all nature goes against you. Rabbits and frogs and all kinds of animals come out of the woods and speak in human tongues and beg you not to do what you intend. Three times you have to turn them away, then they throw in the towel. Next thing you know, the devil comes out and gives you a bag with something awful in it.

The Lord guided Henry through the trees and onto a golf course, a kind of place where Henry had never been in real life. He crossed the sleepy hills, the still waters and sandy places until he witnessed something like a long fat serpent writhing on the ground. Henry squatted in a stand of shrubbery and peeked at the snaky thing, which turned out to be two people trying to fornicate in a sleeping bag.

"Uh, uh, uh," they said.

From what little he could tell it was just the way Henry had imagined it.

There were some sounds of aggravation and then a brief silence.

"It's cold, baby. I'm not getting any blood to it."

"I knew this was a mistake."

The sound of weeping. The whoremonger had made the woman cry. No—it was the *man* crying! A crying man!

"Let me try again. I promise I can do it."

"You had your big chance, junior. I'll tell you one thing. You *will* walk me back to the dorm. And you're not coming in for milk and cookies."

Secular humanists! Henry knew he must be near a state-run college where they tell you it's okay to have abortions and draw the president looking like a monkey.

The man sobbed.

"Where are my pants?" said the woman.

Henry saw the back of a college girl in a golden sweater. There were two portions of her behind like halved peaches dipping below the sweater's hem for all the world to see. And her hair was shorter than the man's!

The man, with the sleeping bag rolled up under his arm, approached the spot where Henry was hiding, so Henry ducked and held his breath.

There was some sniffling and the like, and the woman used the Lord's name in vain and told the man to get a grip, but nobody spotted Henry, and soon there came a spooky silence.

Henry raised his head and saw the sleeping bag jammed in the crook of a small tree.

All was being provided for him.

God was so good!

Henry retrieved the sleeping bag and unrolled it on the ground. He scooted in and zipped it up as far as it would go, leaving only room to breathe. He warmed up quick. The inside of the sleeping bag had a smell that Henry assumed was attempted sexual intercourse. It was pleasant, like a friendly stray dog, and foreboding, like when he had forgotten to clean out his gym locker until the end of the year. It made his pants react. Suddenly he understood everything.

Henry was like Jonah. Jesus had come to him and given him a job to do and Henry had said no, thanks, Lord, not now!

And how about Moses? "Who am I, that I should go unto Pharaoh, and that I should bring forth the children of Israel out of Egypt?"

Everybody had excuses not to follow the Lord.

"Dear God," prayed Henry, "instead of a whale You sent an owl to scare Uncle Lipton into an episode and set me on my path. The Bible doesn't say whale, it says fish. It says a great fish, is I think how You put it. A whale is a mammal, not a fish. A whale's throat would be too small for Jonah because they just eat plankton, which is another proof that the Bible is true. So for that one occasion You made a giant fish. You could have made a whale with a big enough throat I guess but You decided not to and that is good enough for me. Everything happens for a reason. Like the hairs on our arms. Why do we have hairs on our arms? Hairs are sensory devices that help with the senses. Please forgive me for when I said in Bible study I believed in evolution because we have hairs on our arms. So what? Charles Darwin converted on his deathbed. He was like, 'I have totally fouled things up.' He admitted it was all a big mistake. He said he was sorry for messing with people's heads. Now I am sure he is in Heaven because a person could like murder a million people and then accept the Savior into their heart on their deathbed and Jesus will be like, 'Cool.' But that is no excuse to do bad things. You can't be like, 'Ha ha, I am going to kill this person and later on I will ask God to forgive me and I will totally go to Heaven.' That doesn't cut it. Nobody can trick You, Lord. You are not into loopholes. From now on I'm going to do whatever You say. You ordered me to help Polly Finch and I ignored You, Lord. I tried to tell myself I was mistaken. Please forgive me, I thought a demon had tried to fool me by taking Your form. Now I know that was only my foolish rationalizing mind thinking those things, for I was scared to obey Your commandment. I know a demon can take the form of a human person, like when King Saul believed he saw Samuel, but I know now, Lord, that no demon could ever take the shape of You because You would like totally whip them. I should have remembered Your words: 'Thou believest that there is one God; thou doest well: the devils also believe, and tremble.' Even now I can feel the temptation to doubt. Like why would You look like Luke from *The Gilmore Girls*? He is nothing but a big grump and You are so famous for Your positive mental attitude, Lord. Why does he get to date Lorelei? She is so nice. Her eyes are so blue, Lord. If I like anybody I should like Rory, who is more of my own age. But she is just so mopey all the time, Lord, even though she has all the advantages of education and riches, and all that this worldly plane offers, Lord, and she had physical sexual knowingness with Dean even though he was married to that yellow-headed girl. That is when I lost all respect for Rory, Lord. With Your help and strength I will stop watching *The Gilmore Girls* alto- gether, Dear Lord, because now that I am thinking about it everybody on that show is against Your Will and it is not something for a Christian to be watching. But I am not criticizing Your choice of who to look like. And when Luke takes off his cap his hair

looks funny, and I keep thinking why would somebody so beautiful want to date a funny-looking man
like that? But Your hair looked very stylish, Lord. But
anyway maybe You can see why I wondered if it was
really You. I remember what that guy said in chapel
about a little Jesus with laser eyes. I don't want to
judge him, but maybe he was just freaking out. I can't
believe You would shoot lasers out of your eyes
because that would be so unlike You. What else?
Please help Uncle Lipton to get better if that is in
Your eternal plan. If not, well, okay, that's Your call,
but it sure would be a drag. And before I forget, thank
You for providing me with this sleeping bag just as
You provided the Israelites with manna from heaven.
You sent them a pillar of fire to guide them by night
and a pillar of something else to guide them by day, I
can't remember what but maybe it will come back to
me. I'm just like those Israelites because I don't know
where Your commandment will take me, Lord. I don't
know what hardships may lay on the road between
me and Polly Finch. I don't even know where Upstate
New York is, come to think about it. All I can do is
stay alert for any signs You see fit to bring unto me. I
don't expect a pillar of fire, but if You decided to give
me one that would be cool. I would totally love to see

one. Please forgive me for all my sins and protect me on this journey with the presence of Your holy angels. In Jesus's holy and precious name I pray, Amen."

7

"Somebody's been sleeping in my sleeping bag."

Henry woke, nudged by a foot.

"Sorry, mister," he said. He scrambled part way out.

"Mister? How old are you, dude?"

"Fourteen."

"Dude. Me too!"

The boy had kinky black hair instead of straight, his voice was deeper, his complexion was better, and it looked as if he were trying to grow a moustache—but otherwise he might have been Henry's twin.

"So are you like homeless or whatever?"

"Yes," said Henry.

"That sucks. Well, I'm out of here. It's fine if you want to use the sleeping bag or whatever? As long as you don't steal it. I use it to bag these college chicks. They love doing it outside. They're like animals. I'm from New Jersey. They're not like that up there. Up there we got civilization. If I told you what I was doing in that sleeping bag a few minutes ago you wouldn't believe it. Sorry, dude. I'm like wired from doing it so much."

Henry settled back into the sleeping bag.

"Just roll it up and leave it where you found it. Can I trust you, dude?"

"Yes," said Henry.

"Because that's like a hundred-dollar sleeping bag."

The boy held a pack of cigarettes down toward the bag.

"No, thank you," said Henry.

"Dude! You are like one polite homeless person."

The boy lit a cigarette for himself.

"Okay, I better get out of here. Hey, should I like bring you some food tomorrow morning or whatever?"

"No, thank you. I'll be fine."

"Right. Well, you know, take it easy or whatever."

Henry settled down and zipped himself in tight and warm. He heard the boy walking away, and pretty soon he heard him walking back.

"This is stupid. Why don't you come stay at my aunt and uncle's place tonight? You can like sleep in the garage or whatever. There's a space heater. You can get something to eat. You won't rob them or kill them or anything will you?"

"No," said Henry.

"That's cool."

8

They were walking to the aunt and uncle's house.

"I'm staying with them while my parents are in Venezuela monitoring human rights violations," said the boy, whose name was Vince. "My uncle teaches art history at the college. He brings his classes over to the house sometimes and that's how I bag my college chicks. These Southern dudes are too repressed to give them what they want. Like a fourteen-year-old Jersey dude is the equivalent of a twenty-six-year-old Southern dude? That's an estimate."

"My uncle's gone to London, England, with an exploding sore in his brain," said Henry.

"Ouch."

"He's not my uncle. He's my mother's uncle. My great-uncle."

"Yeah, thanks for clearing that up, dude. That's like valuable information. That'll like come in handy if I ever have to write your autobiography."

Vince flicked away his cigarette in an impressive

motion such as Henry had seen in movies about New Jersey.

9

This is what it would be like if there were no moral center. Vince's aunt and uncle had naked pictures on the walls and naked statues on the tables. If something wasn't naked they didn't want anything to do with it. They ate fish for breakfast. On the morning after Vince had rescued Henry from the sleeping bag, Aunt Dora walked around in sweatpants and something like a bra. It was called a "sports bra."

Aunt Dora had been on her way out to run in the city streets halfway naked first thing in the morning when she had noticed Henry watching cartoons with Vince and offered to whip up some breakfast. That was nice of her, but she could have put on a robe or something to cover her nakedness. She was probably about forty and had to wear glasses from infirmity but just flaunted her nakedness unashamed, and the lemony dots in the narrowing pale scoop of her underarm when she reached to get a mixing bowl made Henry weak.

The uncle had a tall, bald forehead but long

orange-and-silver hair in the back, pulled into a ponytail such as was popularized by the forefathers of our nation. He grew a wiry patch under his bottom lip like a drug dealer might have worn and had a silvery devil beard too, and he cursed openly with a big smile on his face in front of young people like it was the most acceptable thing in the world. He put alcohol in his tomato juice in front of everybody.

Neither the aunt nor the uncle objected to the music that Vince blasted through the house during breakfast, rap music in which unhealthy sentiments were endorsed in the filthiest language that Henry had ever heard. The authority figures even pretended to enjoy the rap music. Nobody asked Henry who he was or who his family were or why he was there or when he had shown up because apparently they had abandoned the concepts of responsibility and discipline.

Henry didn't know whether to use a fork or a spoon on any particular thing. Just two years earlier Daphne Bates had seen him pick up a pork chop and eat it with his hands, and that had made the whole year of seventh grade a nightmare. Everybody had started calling him Pork Chop. Some people still did. He used to go home and pray every night that God would erase everybody's memory about the pork chop. It didn't seem like too much to ask compared to making the sun stand still, which God had done one time for Joshua, no problem. Henry finally came to understand that his prayer had been based on pride, which was why it had been answered "no." It wasn't God's fault that Henry had picked up a pork chop with his hands. That was like when these atheists on TV started whining and complaining about "How can God allow a little child to starve?" Hey, I've got an idea, give the child a sandwich and shut up, atheist. In some ways Henry felt that he was no better than an atheist.

"Is everything all right, Henry?"

"Yes, ma'am."

"Well then, go ahead and eat! Don't wait for me. French politeness! Respect for the food!"

Everyone seemed to think that Aunt Dora had made a wonderful comment. All three of them, including Aunt Dora, laughed and laughed. Henry didn't understand. Was it a joke? The French had not supported the war on terrorism. Was it something to do with that? These people probably wished they were in France right now, making fun of the president and going number two on the American flag. He suddenly had an image of the three of them lined up squatting in a row according to height, all laughing and smiling and going number two on a large American flag spread out on the ground. It was an image that was wrong in so many ways. He could see the sandy garden of Aunt Dora's welcoming vulva, for example. Henry asked God to forgive him.

"My goodness, that fellow certainly does want to 'pop a cap' in the posterior region of that 'bee-yotch,' does he not?" said the uncle, referring to the rap performance underway.

Vince shrugged.

"You're one of Vince's 'homeys,' eh, chief?"

"Yes, sir."

"Sir! I find that insulting. Call me Duffy. Everybody else does."

"I don't," said Aunt Dora.

"I don't," said Vince.

"Oh, you guys. You know what I mean. My students do. The 'kids,' or 'home slices' as I refer to them, believe me to be quite 'hep' in that fashion."

"What a loser," said Vince.

"Now, Vince, what have I told you about describing your uncle so accurately?"

Aunt Dora spooned something yellow into a bowl while everyone howled with laughter over her disrespect for the head of the household, and Duffy said a bunch of stuff that apparently came out of an old movie nobody had ever heard of.

Now Henry understood all the pamphlets he had read about why Christian teens should go to Christian colleges when the time arose. Usually if you were a Christian teen and went to a secular university the liberal professors would brainwash you until you thought suicide was normal. Then you'd take drugs and come home for Christmas and shoot your parents.

"Aren't you hungry?" said Aunt Dora.

"Hurt my tongue," said Henry.

"Maybe you could have the polenta," said Aunt Dora.

"Which one's a polenta?" said Henry.

Duffy drained his coffee.

"Sorry," he said, "but I'll have to leave it to you gastronomic explorers to figure that one out. Duty calls."

He got up.

"Where are you going? You don't have class today," said Aunt Dora.

"No, not exactly. Didn't I tell you? I'm taking some of the 'leaders of tomorrow' on a 'real trippy scene.'"

Duffy had promised, it seemed, to drive some of

his students to a special event an hour north of the city, and he had forgotten to tell Aunt Dora, though he could have sworn he had mentioned something.

"You know, Scarecrow Farm," said Duffy.

"I have no idea what you're talking about."

"The guy with all the scarecrows?" said Duffy. "You'll just be bored and uncomfortable and angry. I know how you feel about Brother Lampey."

"I have no idea what you're talking about. But I have a little idea what you're up to."

"Please," said Duffy.

"Where is that again?" said Vince. "That place with the scarecrows?"

"Pineknot," said Duffy. He no longer sounded cheerful. "Pineknot, Alabama. You've never heard of Pineknot, Alabama. Nobody's ever heard of it. Even the people who live there have never heard of it. Are you happy? Is everybody happy? And by the way, can we turn down this music to a *mild roar*?"

"*Ja wohl, mein führer,*" said Aunt Dora.

"That's right, I'm a Nazi."

"Well, you're certainly acting like one."

"Yes, the main thing with the Nazis was they didn't like their music too loud. That's what was wrong with the Nazis. Thank you for the closely reasoned history lesson. Lest we forget."

"Pineknot?" said Vince. "I sure wish I could take Henry there. He's been saying how he wants to get to know the culture of his people. It's a school day, but…"

"You're right, Vince. It's the kind of education you can't get in a school, not in Alabama, anyway," said Aunt Dora. "This is something that means a lot to you, isn't it, Henry?"

Aunt Dora had fed and comforted him—"Or what man is there of you, whom if his son ask bread, will he give him a stone? Or if he ask a fish, will he give him a serpent?"—and it seemed real important to her that Duffy shouldn't leave the house alone.

"Yes, ma'am."

Aunt Dora and Vince tag-teamed Duffy until he caved in because he was so feminized, and then they got Henry dressed for the trip. Aunt Dora dug out some of what she called Duffy's "ancient undergrad duds" to go with Henry's good blue pants—a black turtleneck and a tweed jacket with leather patches on the sleeves. No one asked why he had no normal clothes because the liberal media had turned them too politically correct to judge him.

"There. That's cute. You look just like a little professor," Aunt Dora said to Henry. "A weak, ineffectual little professor."

"That's it. Pick away at my soul, bit by bit," said Duffy.

"What? I was talking to Henry, wasn't I, Henry? Now go have fun."

"That's real Harris tweed," said Duffy. "Look at the label if you don't believe me. That's hand woven in the Outer Hebrides from Scottish-grown wool. It's a collector's item. I don't even know if they make them anymore. We should look it up on the Internet. My mentor gave it to me. Look where he burned a hole in the sleeve. He's dead now."

10

Duffy pouted all the way to the Primate Center.

Henry and Vince rode in the back of the van. Nobody talked.

They pulled up at a medical-looking building of creamy brick. A woman in a white scientist coat and slim rectangular glasses was waiting alone in the portico. Henry heard monkeys hollering and carrying on.

"Hey, Dr. Pogg," said the beautiful young dark-browed scientist.

When she had climbed in and he saw the dreamy black back of her head, Henry knew for certain that she was the girl from the golf course. He studied Vince, who was likewise fixed on her soft dark misting of hair, almost a crewcut, her almost-skull-white scalp beneath it.

"The others couldn't make it, I guess. For the outing," said Duffy.

"What?"

"You remember my nephew."

"Sure…uh…"

"Vince," said Vince. "Surprised to see me?"

The girl laughed in a natural way. "Do you guys mind?" she said, passing her backpack. She smelled like a powerful hand soap that would kill anything. Henry wanted to climb over the seat and get on top of her. Her forehead was bony and exciting, exposed by her short hair and emphasized by her wild eyebrows like a couple of arrows pointing up. It almost looked like they were pointing at a pair of horns under the skin ready to emerge just at the hairline, but not in an evil way.

"And this is Vince's friend Henry. Henry, this is Josie. She's a student in one of my classes. A very gifted student, I might add."

"Hello, ma'am."

"Ma'am! I'm nineteen."

"I'm sorry, ma'am."

"Well, aren't you a little doll."

"We're all little dolls," said Duffy.

11

Twenty more minutes to Pineknot.

Is this where you're leading me, Jesus?

Vince would pick up Josie's backpack and smell it when he thought Henry wasn't looking. Duffy had gotten a weird lump in his throat and he never stopped talking.

"Science is terrific. You know? I mean, I love it. The Age of Enlightenment. Am I boring you? I mean, the internal combustion engine runs on gasoline, thank you very much. How far do you think we could run this baby on prayer? Not very far, I'll tell you that. To put it scientifically, a prayer equals not even one droplet of gasoline. You know? Not one droplet! I would pay a million dollars to a person who could show me a prayer that accomplished even as much as one miniscule droplet of gasoline. Science is just, I don't know, I get excited just wrapping my mind around it. You know? My awesome comprehension of it. Look at that barn. I bet some poor jerk lives over there who thinks he could lay his hands on an empty fuel tank and make a car go. Well, not in the barn. I mean he doesn't live in the barn, of course, but somewhere. He's a type. I shouldn't have mentioned the barn. I'm making a point, okay? You and I, Josie, we understand gravity and so on. The illusion of free will caused by a slight delay of brain waves. They've proven that. We just have the *feeling* we make decisions. That doesn't bother me. I don't need angels playing harps. I enjoy the intricate beauty of physics. Molecules. Entropy. Biological imperatives and so on. Why isn't that enough for people? The glory of a sunset and so on. Because they're stupid, that's why. I'm not telling you anything you don't know, working at the Primate Center among nature's remarkable apes. You know? A sunset can be explained quite rationally without taking away the wonder of it all. Why must mankind turn it into a chariot borne aloft by winged horses? Preposterous! My brain allows me to accept the fact that the earth revolves around the sun and so on, thus producing the lovely sunset. And various meteorological conditions and so on. Is a sunset any less lovely thereby? Of course not. And so, because I side with Galileo or Copernicus or whomever, the village priest is going to ram a hot poker somewhere unpleasant? I am quite relieved to be out of the Dark Ages, thank you very much. But in a way I'm a prisoner of my own wonderful brain, this fantastic computer that no one can understand. Take art. Art is a function of the mind. You know? Expressed through the body. The senses. There's no need to drag religion into it. *Soulful.* What does that mean? It's a word. And all these are words, these various vocally intoned grunts and inflections and so on that I'm using right now. Or are they using *me*? You know? My brain is just dishing them up, one after another with an implacable logic that I am not able to comprehend. And my body is responding by using my vocal chords and tongue and so on, my *soft palate,* et cetera, my uvula I suppose—you as a science major would know better than I!—to manufacture the appropriate physical semblance of the words that my brain is now automatically producing. It's mechanical, is what I'm saying. They've proven it at Harvard. A guy wrote a book. I'm going to get you that book as a personal gift from Amazon dot-com. It just made me think of you somehow. I haven't read it. There was a great article about it somewhere. Hey, maybe I could get us both a copy and we could read it together. We could go somewhere cool and shady and read passages aloud to one another. As part of our tutorial. Wouldn't that be pleasant? What was I talking about?"

"I don't know," said Josie.

"This guy wrote a book proving that there's no free will. That means his body robotically, automatically discovered that it did not possess free will and helplessly, automatically wrote a book about it and somehow found a publisher without being *willing* to find a publisher whatsoever. It's a commendable act of hubris at the very least. Well, to return to my original point, or one of my original points, when you make a work of *art* it doesn't matter what you believe, quote-unquote. What the artist *believes*, quote-unquote, has no bearing on the physical *reality* of the object. The guy with the scarecrows, Brother Lampey? God's not talking to him. There is no God. But because he believes in God he gets to be a quote-unquote *visionary*, quote-unquote. David Hume compared a black man of learning to a parrot that could simulate human speech, did you know that? The father of rationalism! We—white people—we're *human*, he explained with his rationalism, and black people are…something *other*. And John Brown, the religious screwball—I'm talking about a complete nut—*killed and died* for his belief in black *social* equality. You know? Not just *legal* equality, quote-unquote, like almost all the other abolitionists."

"Uh-huh," said Josie.

"What's my point?" said Duffy.

"I really couldn't tell you."

"See? My brain is too aware of itself. It's listening to itself think. Shakespeare could hold two entirely opposite universes in his mind at one time. You know? It's called a dialectic, not to get technical. Have you taken philosophy yet?"

"No."

"You really must."

Suddenly Duffy banged his fists on the steering wheel.

"Aaah!" he said. "I wish I weren't so much like Shakespeare!"

It was Henry's duty as a Christian to witness to Duffy and bring him to the Lord. But Henry's mouth was stopped as if by an angelic presence. "How shall we sing the Lord's song in a strange land?" He could imagine expounding the gospel in a way impossible for Duffy to dispute. Duffy would pull over and everyone would kneel by the roadside. There was a painting of Jesus and the rabbis, Jesus was a blonde kid with an awesome blue hat—Henry wondered if he could get a hat like that at J. Crew—and his robe looked so real you could see the wrinkles and everything.

It looked like that painting in Henry's head, them kneeling by the van and Henry smiling down at them in a powder-blue skullcap, one hand raised as if describing a dove in flight. "Thank you, Henry, for bringing us to Jesus" with tears streaming down their faces and they would go off in the bushes, just Henry and Josie, and Josie would yank down her pants and he could imagine her bunched-up white scientist coat snagged in the briars and bits of gummy pine tree bark sticking to her naked behiney.

Gum was like the living blood that came out of a tree.

For some reason, that thought made Henry feel tender, melancholy, and compassionate, the way Jesus must have felt, and a torrential light filled his hollows.

Their Ancient, Glittering Eyes
by Ron Rash

Because they were boys, no one believed them, including the old men who gathered each morning at the Riverside Gas and Grocery. These retirees huddled by the potbellied stove in rain and cold, on clear days sunning out front like reptiles. The store's middle-aged owner, Cedric Henson, endured their presence with a resigned equanimity. When he'd bought the store five years earlier, Cedric had assumed they were part of the purchase price, in that way no different from the leaky roof and the submerged basement whenever the Tuckaseegee over-spilled its banks.

The two boys, who were brothers, had come clattering across the bridge, red-faced and already holding their arms apart as if carrying huge, invisible packages. They stood gasping a few moments, waiting for enough breath to tell what they'd seen.

"This big," the twelve-year-old said, his arms

spread wide apart as he could stretch them.

"No, even bigger," the younger boy said.

Cedric had been peering through the screen door but now stepped outside.

"What you boys talking about?" he asked.

"A fish," the older boy said, "in the pool below the bridge."

Rudisell, the oldest of the three at eighty-nine, expertly delivered a squirt of tobacco between himself and the boys. Creech and Campbell simply nodded at each other knowingly. Time had vanquished them to the role of spectators in the world's affairs, and from their perspective the world both near and far was now controlled by fools. The causes of this devolution dominated their daily conversations. The octogenarians Rudisell and Campbell blamed Franklin Roosevelt and fluoridated water. Creech, a mere seventy-six, leaned toward Elvis Presley and television.

"The biggest fish ever come out of the Tuckaseegee was a thirty-one-inch brown trout caught in nineteen and forty-eight," Rudisell announced to all present. "I seen it weighed in this very store. Fifteen pounds and two ounces."

The other men nodded in confirmation.

"This fish was twice bigger than that," the younger boy challenged.

The boy's impudence elicited another spray of tobacco juice from Rudisell.

"Must be a whale what swum up from the ocean," Creech said. "Though that's a long haul. It'd have to come up the Gulf Coast and the Mississippi, for the water this side of the mountain flows west."

"Could be one of them log fish," Campbell offered. "They get that big. Them rascals will grab your bait and then turn into a big chunk of wood afore you can set the hook."

"They's snakes all over that pool, even some copperheads," Rudisell warned. "You younguns best go somewhere else to make up your tall tales."

The smaller boy pooched out his lower lip as if about to cry.

"Come on," his brother said. "They ain't going to believe us." The boys walked back across the road to the bridge. The old men watched as the boys leaned over the railing, took a last look before climbing atop their bicycles and riding away.

"Fluoridated water," Rudisell wheezed. "Makes them see things."

On the following Saturday morning, Harley

Wease scrambled up the same bank the boys had, carrying the remnants of his Zebco 202. Harley's hands trembled as he laid the shattered rod and reel on the ground before the old men. He pulled out a soiled handkerchief from his jeans and wiped his bleeding index finger to reveal a deep slice between the first and second joints. The old men studied the finger and the rod and reel and awaited explanation. They were attentive, for Harley's deceased father had been a close friend of Rudisell's.

"Broke my rod like it was made of balsa wood," Harley said. "Then the gears on the reel got stripped. It got down to just me and the line pretty quick." Harley raised his index finger so the men could see it better. "I figured to use my finger for the drag. If the line hadn't broke, you'd be looking at a nub."

"You sure it was a fish?" Campbell asked. "Maybe you caught hold of a muskrat or snapping turkle."

"Not unless them critters has got to where they grow fins," Harley said.

"You saying it was a trout?" Creech asked.

"I only got a glimpse, but it didn't look like no trout. Looked like a alligator but for the fins."

"I never heard of no such fish in Jackson County," Campbell said, "but Rudy Nicholson's boys seen the same. It's pretty clear there's *something* in that pool."

The men turned to Rudisell for his opinion.

"I don't know what it is either," Rudisell said. "But I aim to find out."

Rudisell lifted the weathered ladder-back chair, held it aloft shakily as he made his slow way across the road to the bridge. Harley went into the store to talk with Cedric, but the other two men followed Rudisell as if all were deposed kings taking their thrones into some new kingdom. They lined their chairs up at the railing. They waited.

Only Creech had undiminished vision, but in the coming days that was rectified. Campbell had not thought anything beyond five feet of himself worth viewing for years, but now a pair of thick, round-lensed spectacles adorned his head, giving him a look of owlish intelligence. Rudisell had a spyglass he claimed had once belonged to a German U-boat captain. The bridge was now effectively one lane, but traffic tended to be light. While trucks and cars drove around them, the old men kept vigil morning to evening, retreating into the store only when rain came.

Vehicles sometimes paused on the bridge to ask

for updates, because the lower half of Harley Wease's broken rod had become an object of great wonder since being mounted on Cedric's back wall. Boys and men frequently took it down to grip the hard plastic handle. They invariably pointed the jagged fiberglass in the direction of the bridge, held it out as if a divining rod that might yet give some measure or resonance of what had made the pool its lair.

Rudisell spotted the fish first. A week had passed with daily rains clouding the river, but two days of sun settled the silt, the shallow tailrace clear all the way to the bottom. This was where Rudisell aimed his spyglass, setting it on the rail to steady his aim. He made a slow sweep of the sandy floor every fifteen minutes. Many things came into focus as he adjusted the scope: a flurry of nymphs rising to become mayflies, glints of fool's gold, schools of minnows shifting like migrating birds, crayfish with pincers raised as if surrendering to the behemoth sharing the pool with them.

It wasn't there, not for hours, but then it was. At first Rudisell saw just a shadow over the white sand, slowly gaining depth and definition, and then the slow wave of the gills and pectoral fins, the shudder of the tail as the fish held its place in the current.

"I see it," Rudisell whispered, "in the tailrace." Campbell took off his glasses and grabbed the spyglass, placed it against his best eye as Creech got up slowly, leaned over the rail.

"Long as my leg," Creech said.

"That thing's big as a alligator," Campbell uttered.

"I never thought to see such a thing," Rudisell said.

The fish held its position a few more moments, then slowly moved into deeper water.

"I never seen the like of a fish like that," Creech announced.

"It ain't a trout," Campbell said.

"Nor carp or bass," Rudisell added.

"Maybe it is a gator," Campbell said. "One of them snowbirds from Florida could of put it in there."

"No," Rudisell said. "I seen gators during my army training in Louisiana. A gator's like us, it's got to breathe air. This thing don't need air. Beside, it had a tail fin."

"Then maybe it's a mermaid," Creech mused.

By late afternoon the bridge looked like an overloaded barge. Pickups, cars, and two tractors clotted both sides of the road and the store's parking lot.

Men and boys squirmed and shifted to get a place against the railing. Harley Wease recounted his epic battle, but it was the ancients who were most deferred to as they made pronouncements about size and weight. Of species they could only speak by negation.

"My brother works down at that nuclear power plant near Walhalla," Marcus Price said. "Billy swears there's catfish below the dam near five foot long. Claims that radiation makes them bigger."

"This ain't no catfish," Rudisell said. "It didn't have no big jug-head. More lean than that."

Bascombe Greene ventured the shape called to mind the pike-fish caught in weedy lakes up north. Stokes Hamilton thought it could be a hellbender salamander, for though he'd never seen one more than twelve inches long he'd heard tell they got to six feet in Japan. Leonard Coffey told a long, convoluted story about a goldfish set free in a pond. After two decades of being fed cornbread and fried okra, the fish had been caught and it weighed fifty-seven pounds.

"It ain't no pike nor spring lizard nor goldfish," Rudisell said emphatically.

"Well, there's but one way to know," Bascombe Greene said, "and that's to try and catch the damn thing." Bascombe nodded at Harley. "What bait was you fishing with?"

Harley looked sheepish.

"I'd lost my last spinner when I snagged a limb. All I had left in my tackle box was a rubber worm I use for bass, so I put it on."

"What size and color?" Bascombe asked. "We got to be scientific about this."

"Seven inch," Harley said. "It was purple with white dots."

"You got any more of them?" Leonard Coffey asked.

"No, but you can buy them at Sylva Hardware."

"Won't do you no good," Rudisell said.

"Why not?" Leonard asked.

"For a fish to live long enough to get that big it's got to be smart. It'll not forget that a rubber worm tricked it."

"It might not be near smart as you reckon," Bascombe said. "I don't mean no disrespect, but old folks tend to be forgetful. Maybe that old fish is the same way."

"I reckon we'll know the truth of that soon enough," Rudisell concluded, because fishermen were already casting from the bridge and banks. Soon several lines had gotten tangled, and a fistfight broke out over who had claim to a choice spot near the pool's tailrace. More people arrived as the afternoon wore on, became early evening. Cedric, never one to miss a potential business opportunity, put a plastic fireman's hat on his head and a whistle in his mouth. He parked cars while his son Bobby crossed and recrossed the bridge selling Cokes from a battered shopping cart.

Among the later arrivals was Charles Meekins, the county's game warden. He was thirty-eight years old and had grown up in Cambridge, Massachusetts. The general consensus, especially among the old men, was that the warden was arrogant and a smart-ass. Meekins stopped often at the store, and he invariably addressed them as Wynken, Blynken, and Nod. He now listened with undisguised condescension as the old men, Harley, and finally the two boys told of what they'd seen.

"It's a trout or carp," Meekins said, "carp" sounding like "cop." Despite four years in Jackson County, Meekins still spoke as if his vocal cords had been pulled from his throat and reinstalled in his sinus cavity. "There's no fish larger in these waters."

Harley handed his reel to the game warden.

"That fish stripped the gears on it."

Meekins inspected the reel as he might an obviously fraudulent fishing license.

"You probably didn't have the drag set right."

"It was bigger than any trout or carp," Campbell insisted.

"When you're looking into water you can't really judge the size of something," Meekins said. He looked at some of the younger men and winked, "especially if your vision isn't all that good to begin with."

A palmful of Red Mule chewing tobacco bulged the right side of Rudisell's jaw like a tumor, but his apoplexy was such that he swallowed a portion of his cud and began hacking violently. Campbell slapped him on the back and Rudisell spewed dark bits of tobacco onto the bridge's wooden flooring. Meekins had gotten back in his green Fish and Wildlife truck before Rudisell had recovered enough to speak.

"If I hadn't near choked to death I'd have told that shit-britches youngun to bend over and we'd see if my sight was good enough to ram this spyglass up his ass."

In the next few days so many fishermen came to try their luck that Rudisell finally bought a wire-bound notebook from Cedric and had anglers sign up for fifteen-minute slots. They cast almost every offering imaginable into the pool. A good half of the anglers succumbed to the theory that what had worked before could work again, so rubber worms were the single most popular choice. The rubber-worm devotees used an array of different sizes, hues, and even smells. Some went with seven-inch rubber worms while others favored five- or ten-inch. Some tried worms purple with white dots while others tried white with purple dots and still others tried pure white and pure black and every variation between including chartreuse, pink, turquoise, and fuchsia. Some used rubber worms with auger tails and others used flat tails. Some worms smelled like motor oil and some worms smelled like strawberries and some worms had no smell at all.

The others were divided by their devotion to live bait or artificial lures. Almost all the bait fisherman used night crawlers and red worms in the belief that if the fish had been fooled by an imitation, the actual live worm would work even better, but they also cast spring lizards, minnows, crickets, grubs, wasp larvae, crawfish, frogs, newts, toads, and even a live field mouse. The lure contingent favored spinners of the Panther Martin and Roostertail variety though they were not averse to Rapalas, Jitterbugs, Hula Poppers,

Johnson Silver Minnows, Devilhorses, and a dozen other hook-laden pieces of wood or plastic. Some lures sank and bounced along the bottom and some lures floated and still others gurgled and rattled and some made no sound at all and one lure even changed colors depending on depth and water temperature. Jarvis Hampton cast a Rapala F 14 he'd once caught a tarpon with in Florida. A subgroup of fly fishermen cast Muddler Minnows, Wooly Boogers, Wooly Worms, Royal Coachmen, streamers and wet flies, nymphs and dry flies, and some hurled nymphs and dry flies together that swung overhead like miniature bolas.

During the first two days five brown trout, one speckled trout, one ball cap, two smallmouth bass, ten knottyheads, a bluegill, and one old boot were caught. A gray squirrel was snagged by an errant cast into a tree. Neither the squirrel nor the various fish outweighed the boot, which weighed one pound and eight ounces after the water was poured out. On the third day Wesley McIntire's rod doubled and the drag whirred. A rainbow trout leaped in the pool's center, Wesley's quarter-ounce Panther Martin spinner embedded in its upper jaw. He fought the trout for five minutes before his brother Robbie could net it.

The rainbow was twenty-two inches long and weighed five and a half pounds, big enough that Wesley took it straight to the taxidermist to be mounted.

Charles Meekins came by an hour later. He didn't get out of the truck, just rolled down his window and nodded. His radio played loudly, and the atonal guitars and screeching voices made Rudisell glad he was mostly deaf because hearing only part of the racket made him feel like stinging wasps were locked inside his head. Meekins didn't bother to turn the radio down, just shouted over the music.

"I told you it was a trout."

"That wasn't it," Rudisell shouted. "The fish I seen could of eaten that rainbow for breakfast."

Meekins smiled, showing a set of bright-white teeth that, unlike Rudisell's, did not have to be deposited in a glass jar every night.

"Then why didn't it? That rainbow has probably been in that pool for years." Meekins shook his head. "I wish you old boys would learn to admit when you're wrong about something."

Meekins rolled up his window as Rudisell pursed his lips and fired a stream of tobacco juice directly at Meekins' left eye. The tobacco hit the glass and dribbled a dark, phlegmy rivulet down the window.

"A fellow such as that ought not be allowed a guvment uniform," Creech said.

"Not unless it's got black-and-white stripes all up and down it," Crenshaw added.

After ten days no other fish of consequence had been caught and anglers began giving up. The notebook was discarded because appointments were no longer necessary. Meekins's belief gained credence, especially since in ten days none of the hundred or so men and boys who'd gathered there had seen the giant fish.

"I'd be hunkered down on the stream bottom, too, if such commotion was going on around me," Creech argued, but few remained to nod in agreement. Even Harley Wease began to have doubts.

"Maybe that rainbow *was* what I had on," he said heretically.

By the first week in May only the old men remained on the bridge. They kept their vigil, but the occupants of cars and trucks and tractors no longer paused to ask about sightings. When the fish reappeared in the tailrace, the passing drivers ignored the old men's frantic waves to come see. They drove across the bridge with eyes fixed straight ahead, embarrassed by their elders' dementia.

"That's the best look we've gotten yet," Campbell said when the fish moved out of the shallows and into deeper water. "It's six feet long if it's a inch."

Rudisell set his spyglass on the bridge railing and turned to Creech, the one among them who still had a car and driver's license.

"You got to drive me over to Jarvis Hampton's house," Rudisell said.

"What for?" Creech asked.

"Because we're going to rent out that rod and reel he uses for them tarpon. Then we got to go by the library, because I want to know what this thing is when we can catch it."

Creech kept the speedometer at a steady thirty-five as they followed the river south to Jarvis Hampton's farm. They found Jarvis in his tobacco field and quickly negotiated a ten-dollar-a-week rental for the rod and reel, four 2/0 vanadium-steel fish hooks, and four sinkers. Jarvis offered a net as well but Rudisell claimed it wasn't big enough for what they were after. "But I'll take a hay hook and a whetstone if you got it," Rudisell added, "and some bailing twine and a feed sack."

They packed the fishing equipment in the trunk

and drove to the county library where they used Campbell's library card to check out an immense tome called *Freshwater Fish of North America.* The book was so heavy that only Creech had the strength to carry it, holding it before him with both hands as if the book were made of stone. He dropped it in the backseat and, still breathing heavily, got behind the wheel and cranked the engine.

"We got one more stop," Rudisell said, "that old mill pond on Spillcorn Creek."

"You wanting to practice with that rod and reel?" Campbell asked.

"No, to get our bait," Rudisell replied. "I been thinking about something. After that fish hit Harley's rubber worm they was throwing night crawlers right and left into the pool thinking that fish thought Harley's lure was a worm. But what if it thought that rubber worm was something else, something we ain't seen one time since we been watching that pool though it used to be thick with them?"

Campbell understood first.

"I get what you're saying, but this is one bait I'd rather not be gathering myself, or putting on a hook for that matter."

"Well, if you'll just hold the sack I'll do the rest."

"What about baiting the hook?"

"I'll do that, too."

Since the day was warm and sunny, a number of reptiles had gathered on the stone slabs that had once been a dam. Most were blue-tailed skinks and fence lizards, but several mud-colored serpents coiled sullenly on the largest stones. Creech, who was deathly afraid of snakes, remained in the car. Campbell carried the burlap feed sack, reluctantly trailing Rudisell through broom sedge to the old dam.

"Them snakes ain't of the poisonous persuasion?" Campbell asked.

Rudisell turned and shook his head.

"Naw. Them's just your common water snake. Mean as the devil but they got no fangs."

As they got close the skinks and lizards darted for crevices in the rocks, but the snakes did not move until Rudisell's shadow fell over them. Three slithered away before Rudisell's creaky back could bend enough for him to grab hold, but the fourth did not move until Rudisell's liver-spotted hand closed around its neck. The snake thrashed violently, its mouth biting at the air. Campbell reluctantly moved closer, his fingers and thumbs holding the sack open, arms extended out from his body as if attempting to catch some object falling from the sky. As soon as Rudisell stuffed it in, Campbell gave the snake and sack to Rudisell, who knotted the burlap and put it in the trunk.

"You figure one to be enough?" Campbell asked.

"Yes," Rudisell replied. "We'll get but one chance."

The sun was beginning to settle over Balsam Mountain when the old men got back to the bridge. Rudisell led them down the path to the riverbank, the feed sack in his right hand, the hay hook and twine in his left. Campbell came next with the rod and reel and sinkers and hooks. Creech came last, the great book clutched to his chest. The trail was steep and narrow, the weave of leaf and limb overhead so thick it seemed they were entering a cave.

Once they got to the bank and caught their breath, they went to work. Creech used two of the last teeth left in his head to clamp three sinkers onto the line, then tied the hook to the monofilament with an expertly rendered hangman's knot. Campbell studied the book and found the section on fish living in southeastern rivers. He folded the page where the photographs of relevant fish began and then marked the back section where corresponding printed information was located. Rudisell took out the whetstone and sharpened the metal with the same attentiveness as the long-ago warriors who'd once roamed these hills honed their weapons, those bronze men who'd flaked dull stone to make their flesh-piercing arrowheads. Soon the steel tip shone like silver.

"All right, I done my part," Creech said when he'd tested the drag. He eyed the writhing feed sack apprehensively. "I ain't about to be close by when you try to get that snake on that hook."

Creech moved over near the tailwaters as Campbell picked up the rod and reel. He settled the rod tip above Rudisell's head, the fish hook dangling inches from the older man's beaky nose. Rudisell unknotted the sack, then pinched the fishhook's eye between his left hand's index finger and thumb, used the right to slowly peel back the burlap. When the snake was exposed, Rudisell grabbed it by the neck, stuck the fish hook through the midsection, and quickly let go. The rod tip sagged with the snake's weight as Creech moved farther down the bank.

"What do I do now?" Campbell shouted, for the snake was swinging in an arc that brought the serpent ever closer to his body.

"Cast it," Rudisell replied.

Campbell made a frantic sideways, two-handed

heave that looked more like someone throwing a tub of dishwater off a back porch than a cast. The snake landed three feet from the bank, but luck was with them for the snake began swimming toward the pool's center. Creech had come back to stand by Campbell, but his eyes were on the snake, ready to flee up the bank if it took a mind to change direction. Rudisell gripped the hay hook's handle in his right hand. With his left he began wrapping bailing twine around metal and flesh. The wooden bridge floor rumbled like low thunder as a pickup crossed. A few seconds later another vehicle passed over the bridge. Rudisell continued wrapping the twine. He had no watch but suspected it was after five and men working in Sylva were starting to come home. When Rudisell used up all the twine, he had Creech knot it.

"With that hay hook tied to you it looks like you're the bait," Creech joked.

"If I gaff that thing it's not going to get free of me," Rudisell vowed.

The snake was past the deepest part of the pool now, making steady progress toward the far bank. It struggled to the surface briefly, the weight of the sinkers pulling it back down. The line did not move for a few moments, then began a slow movement back toward the heart of the pool.

"Why you figure it to turn around?" Campbell asked as Creech took a first step farther up the bank.

"I don't know," Rudisell said. "Why don't you tighten your line a bit."

Campbell turned the handle twice and the monofilament grew taut and the rod tip bent. "Damn snake's got hung up."

"Give it a good jerk and it'll come free," Creech said. "Probably just tangled in some brush."

Campbell yanked upward, and the rod bowed. The line began moving upstream, not fast but steady, the reel chattering as the monofilament stripped off.

"It's on," Campbell said softly, as if afraid to startle the fish.

The line did not pause until it was thirty yards upstream and in the shadow of the bridge.

"You got to turn it," Rudisell shouted, "or it'll wrap that line around one of them pillars."

"Turn it," Campbell replied. "I can't even slow it down."

But the fish turned of its own volition, headed back into the deeper water. For fifteen minutes the creature sulked on the pool's bottom. Campbell kept the rod bowed, breathing hard as he strained against the immense weight on the other end. Finally, the fish began moving again, over to the far bank and then upstream. Campbell's arms began trembling violently.

"My arms is give out," he said and handed the rod to Creech. Campbell sprawled out on the bank, his chest heaving rapidly, limbs shaking as if palsied. The fish swam back into the pool's heart and another ten minutes passed. Rudisell looked up at the bridge. Cars and trucks continued to rumble across. Several vehicles paused a few moments but no faces appeared at the railing.

Creech tightened the drag and the rod bent double.

"Easy," Rudisell said. "You don't want him breaking off."

"The way it's going, it'll kill us all before it gets tired," Creech gasped.

The additional pressure worked. The fish moved again, this time allowing the line in its mouth to lead it into the tailrace. For the first time they saw the fish.

"Lord'amercy," Campbell exclaimed, for what they saw was over six feet long and enclosed by a brown suit of armor, the immense tail curved like a scythe. It looked prehistoric. When the fish saw the old men it surged away, the drag chattering again as it moved back into the deeper water.

Rudisell sat down beside the book and rapidly turned pages of color photos until he saw it.

"It's a sturgeon," he shouted, then rapidly turned to where the printed information was, began to call out bursts of information. "Can grow over seven feet long and three hundred pounds. That stuff that looks like armor is called scutes. They's even got a Latin name here. Says they was once in near every river, but now endangered. Can live a hundred and fifty years."

"I ain't going to live another hundred and fifty seconds if I don't get some relief," Creech said and handed the rod back to Campbell.

Campbell took over as Creech collapsed on the bank. The sturgeon began to give ground, the reel handle making slow, clockwise revolutions.

Rudisell closed the book and stepped into the shallows of the pool's tailrace. A sandbar formed a few yards out and that was what he moved toward, the hay hook raised like a metal question mark. Once he'd secured himself on the sandbar, Rudisell turned to Campbell.

"Lead him over here. There's no way we can lift him up the bank."

"You gonna try to gill that thing?" Creech asked incredulously.

Rudisell shook his head.

"I ain't gonna gill it, I'm going to stab this hay hook in so deep it'll have to drag me back into that pool with it to get away."

The reel handle turned quicker now, and soon the sturgeon came out of the depths, emerging like a submarine. Campbell moved farther down the bank, only three or four yards from the sandbar. Creech had gotten up and now stood beside Campbell. The fish came straight toward them, face first as if led on a leash. They could see the head clearly now, the cone-shaped snout, barbels hanging beneath the snout like whiskers. As it came closer Rudisell creakily kneeled down on the sandbar's edge. As he swung the hay hook downward the sturgeon made a last surge toward deeper water. The bright metal raked across the scaly back but did not penetrate.

"Damn," Rudisell swore.

"You got to beach it," Creech shouted at Campbell, who began reeling again, not pausing until the immense head was half out of the water, snout touching the sandbar. The sturgeon's wide mouth opened, revealing an array of rusting hooks and lures that hung from the lips like medals.

"Gaff it now," Creech shouted.

"Hurry," Crenshaw huffed, the rod in his hands doubled like a bow. "I'm herniating myself."

But Rudisell appeared not to hear them. He stared intently at the fish, the hay hook held overhead as if it were a torch allowing him to see the sturgeon more clearly.

Rudisell's blue eyes brightened for a moment, and an enigmatic smile creased his face. The hay hook's sharpened point flashed, aimed not at the fish but the monofilament. A loud twang like a broken guitar string sounded across the water. The rod whipped back and Campbell stumbled backwards but Creech caught him before he fell. The sturgeon was motionless for a few moments, then slowly curved back toward the pool's heart. As it disappeared, Rudisell remained kneeling on the sandbar, his eyes gazing into the pool. Campbell and Creech staggered over to the bank and sat down.

"They'll never believe us," Creech said, "not in a million years, especially that smart-ass game warden."

"We had it good as caught," Campbell muttered. "We *had* it caught."

None of them spoke further for a long while, each exhausted by the battle. But their silence had more to do with each man's self-reflection on what he had just witnessed than weariness. A yellow mayfly rose like a watery spark in the tailrace, hung in the air a few moments before it fell and was swept away by the current. As time passed crickets announced their presence on the bank, and downriver a whippoorwill called. More mayflies rose in the tailrace. The air became chilly as the sheltering trees closed more tightly around them, absorbed the waning sun's light, a preamble to another overdue darkness.

"It's okay," Campbell finally said.

Creech looked at Rudisell, who still was on the sandbar. "You done the right thing. I didn't see that at first, but I see it now."

Rudisell finally stood up, wiped the wet sand from the knees of his pants. As he stepped into the shallows he saw something in the water. He picked it up and put it in his pocket.

"Find you a fleck of gold?" Campbell asked.

"Better than gold," Rudisell replied, and joined his comrades on the bank.

They could hardly see their own feet as they walked up the path to the bridge. As they emerged they found the green Fish and Wildlife truck parked at the trail end. The passenger window was down and Meekins' smug face looked out at them.

"So you old boys haven't drowned after all. Folks saw the empty chairs and figured you'd fallen in."

Meekins nodded at the fishing equipment in Campbell's hands and smiled.

"Have any luck catching your monster?"

"Caught it and let it go," Campbell said.

"That's mighty convenient," Meekins said. "I don't suppose anyone else actually saw this giant fish, or that you have a photograph."

"No," Creech said serenely. "But it's way bigger than you are."

Meekins shook his head. He no longer smiled. "Must be nice to have nothing better to do than make up stories, but this is getting old real quick."

Rudisell stepped up to the truck's window, only inches away from Meekins's face when he raised his hand. A single diamond-shaped object was wedged between Rudisell's gnarled index finger and thumb. Though tinted brown, it appeared to be translucent. He held it eye level in front of Meekins's face as if it were a silty monocle they both might peer through.

"*Acipenser fulvescens,*" Rudisell said, the Latin

uttered slowly as if an incantation. He put the scute back in his pocket, and without further acknowledgment of Meekins's existence stepped around the truck and onto the hardtop. Campbell followed with the fishing equipment and Creech came last with the book. It was a slow, dignified procession. They walked westward toward the store, the late-afternoon sun burnishing their cracked and wasted faces. Coming out of the shadows, they blinked their eyes as if dazzled, much in the manner of old-world saints who have witnessed the blinding brilliance of the one true vision.

HATTIESBURG, MISSISSIPPI
by James Whorton Jr.

HATTIESBURG, MISSISSIPPI.
Not the easiest town to be a poet in!

To prove it I cite my entire body of work. It consists of only one poem, which I actually didn't write but plagiarized. The world will never know what wonders of unplagiarized poetry I might have given it, if only I'd had the good fortune to be raised in a place that is friendlier to poets than Hattiesburg, Mississippi.

Afghanistan, for example.

The ways in which an aspiring poet in Hattiesburg is made to feel discouraged are many. In my senior year of high school, Leslie Ann Jeter's parents sued the school board because their daughter had been made to read the butt-kissing scene from "The Miller's Tale" out loud in class. Miriam Vaughn, our English teacher, had warned us of what she termed "the blue passages" and said we were at liberty to skip over them; therefore, as Mrs. Vaughn held, and as I also believed, it was Leslie Ann's own fault that she had read out the butt-kissing. Dentist and Mrs. Jeter, however, felt that because their daughter spoke the language of South Mississippi in 1985—a version of Modern English—and not the language of London in 1385 (referred to as Middle English), their daughter had not known nor could she have been expected to know what she was reading until Mrs. Vaughn, whose pleasure was evident to everyone, translated the controversial passage for all to understand.

I was there in class when it happened and do remember it vividly, as anyone would who ever saw a girl as white as Leslie Ann turn as pink as she did on that day. She'd been doing her schoolgirl darnedest to follow the five rules of Middle English pronunciation from Mrs. Vaughn's handout while at the same time observing our local custom of diphthonging every individual vowel.

> *Dairk woss the neegt oss peech or oss the cowela,*
>
> *Ond ott the weeyundoo oot shay poota heer howela*
>
> *Ond Obsolown, heeyum feel no bait nay wayers,*

Boot weeth hees mooth hay keesta heer nokked
   ayers.

Leslie Ann blinked innocently, like a kitten.

It could have ended there, but my friend Alison Cartwright, who understood Middle English, put both hands over her face. She was not a prude, but she did happen to share her first name with the hussy in Chaucer's story who had just put her *howela* out the *weeyundoo.*

Mrs. Vaughn asked Alison why she was blushing.

"I'm not blushing," Alison said from behind her hands.

Alison didn't like to speak in class. She wore a brace under her shirt to correct her scoliosis, which made her self-conscious.

Mrs. Vaughn translated, smiling grandly, without hurrying. Lisa Stringer, who was far and away the most beautiful girl in our school—an athletic, golden, frolicsome, cheerful girl with round, wide-awake eyes and big brown irises, whose smooth jeans did not so much clothe her graceful form as describe it, lovingly, with painstaking precision and fidelity to nature—and who was affable and pleasant with everyone, even a mole like myself, because she was gorgeous enough to afford it: she had wealth to spare—Lisa Stringer was the first to bust out laughing, and the rest of the class followed, including Leslie Ann! Yes, Leslie Ann turned pink—much pinker than Alison had. It was a deep, warm pink, almost magenta—the color of exposure itself! But she laughed with the rest of us, as though the notion of her reading that bit about Absolon kissing Alison's butt was just the funniest thing she had ever encountered in all her protected and stainless days.

On the inside, though, Leslie Ann was burning! In fact, I suspect it was not the reading that humiliated her so badly she had to seek legal redress, but her own helpless laughter. She had let the situation get ahead of her, and in that sense—figuratively, as it were—it was her own ass she had shown. If only she had studied a lot harder, and known that the part about the butts was in there—then when Mrs. Vaughn translated it she would have responded not with honest laughter but with the decent, composed, pert little frown that was her specialty.

Oh, the dirtiness and shame!

And the chilling effect took its toll. If the lines of Geoffrey Chaucer, whose body reposed alongside those of Tennyson and Dr. Johnson in the Poet's Corner of Westminster Abbey, were too grisly and too hard-hitting for Hattiesburg, Mississippi, then what was the point of my even trying? I certainly wasn't interested in churning out the kind of flavorless baby food that would suit the moralizing, disapproving, school-board-suing, out-of-court-settling Leslie Ann Jeters of the world, and her parents. I would have refused to write such pabulum even if my extra-strong gag reflex permitted me to attempt it, which I don't think it would've.

Not to mention that, as far as I could tell, there was nothing going on in Hattiesburg worth writing a poem about anyway.

I shared this observation with Alison when we were talking on the phone.

"I wrote a poem about something that happened in Hattiesburg," she said.

"You wrote a poem? Let me read it," I said.

"I will if you let me read one of yours," she said.

"Sorry," I said. "Nobody reads my poems."

We were quiet awhile. I was lying on my bed, watching the ceiling fan. My ear was hot, so I moved the phone to the other side of my head.

I confessed to her that I had never actually finished a poem.

"Finish one and show it to me, and I will show

you mine," she said.

"Okay," I said.

Then she asked me if I wanted to boycott the whites-only spring formal with her. In Hattiesburg we didn't have a regular high school prom, because if the high school had given a prom it would have had to be integrated. Instead, some white parents rented the community center and put on a dance that was by invitation only.

"Sure, I'll boycott it with you," I said. "Are you going to picket, or just not show up?"

"I have to show up and then leave," she said. "Otherwise people will assume I couldn't get a date."

"You could get a date," I said.

That night I became frantic and nearly beat my brains out trying to write a poem. In my blue 1984 Honda Civic hatchback that my parents had given me I drove up and down the whole length of Hardy Street—the whole width of Hattiesburg—back and forth, like an insane gerbil shuttling in its cage. Burgertown, with its rows of small orange lights! The Gold Post; the Hardy Street Cinema! Nothing had ever changed on this street. The whole thing had always been exactly this way, and it would always continue to be exactly so. The Triangle Food Store;

Rose's discount variety; The Mexican Kitchen; the campus of the University of Southern Mississippi, with its soul-numbing rose garden and duck pond: these did not inspire me! I tried to pretend I was somewhere else. Greenwich Village in the seventies! Greenwich Village in the fifties! I drove through Taco Bell for a 59-cent burrito, and then I drove home, still poemless. Defeated, I slipped between the taut, detergent-scented sheets of my bed and lay in the dark with my thoughts careening as the air-conditioner cycled on and off. Whenever it clicked on, I could hear my hollow bedroom door shift against the jamb.

On the night of the spring formal I showed up at Alison's house with a corsage in a clear plastic to-go box. Her mother snatched it from my hands in the foyer and pinned it to the green satin bosom of Alison's gown while I watched. Alison was a thin girl, long-limbed, freckled, with pretty, sorrel-colored hair and eyebrows that were a couple of shades darker. She had her brace on under the gown. I was wearing a dark suit bothered, I mean borrowed, from my father. Mrs. Cartwright rather brusquely pinned an orchid to my lapel, and then she made us stand with our backs to the front door and took our picture. Alison's father didn't appear. I had never met him.

Here is how people danced, at those dances in Hattiesburg in the eighties. Everyone formed into two lines, facing, and you stepped from one foot to the other, bouncing a little if you felt the need and maybe pointing a finger now and then for punctuation. There wasn't a great deal of exuberance or spontaneity in the native dance of predominantly Baptist Hattiesburg, Mississippi. There was one rather hysterical exchange student who would sometimes lift both arms over her head and spin around completely—it was a move she'd brought along from her homeland of Bavaria, and at the end of our senior year she took it back with her.

It was dark in the community center, with flashes and booming bass. We didn't leave right away but ate some refreshments and stood talking with some of the other hard cases: George Buckley, Sara Chang, Ann Pestle, Lance Fayard, Ellen O'Rourke—the sweet gang of nerds, of whom we were two. I was bored and anxious. Everybody wants to be popular in high school, right? It stings when you're not. And you know you should be caring about other things, because what could be more absurd than a bunch of middle-class white kids standing around in formal wear feeling sorry that they are not better-liked?

There was Lisa Stringer, stepping from foot to foot gazing fondly into the stupid eyes of her Paul Bunyan–like boyfriend, who was a Rear End or a Full Receiver or something like that.

Leslie Ann Jeter was there too, in a dress made out of umbrella fabric.

Alison and I left the dance quietly and went to the Jr. Food Mart. I got a Chick-O-Stick and Alison sorted through the Necco wafers to find the pack that had the fewest orange ones in it. Then we drove to the First Mississippi Bank parking garage to trade poems.

She showed me hers first. It was a poem about making pancakes with her three-year-old cousin. It was OK—I didn't like it very much, and I told her it sort of proved my point that there was nothing going on in Hattiesburg to inspire serious verse.

She smiled at me. She had one of those smiles where you can see the pink line of the gums on top, above the teeth. Not a cool or reserved smile but a friendly, happy one.

I wondered why we were here. Our walk-out hadn't caused much of a scene at the community center. They didn't even stop dancing. I asked Alison what kind of a boycott this was, and she shrugged. "My mother wanted a picture of me in this dress," she said. "It's my senior year."

I think I may have grunted.

She asked to see my poem now.

"I plagiarized it from Chaucer," I said.

"Let me see it," she said.

I handed it over.

"'Alison,'" she said. That was the title of my poem—"Alison."

She read it out loud.

Only eighteen summers old,

Alison was uncontrolled.

Long as a mast, straight as a bolt,

Winsome as a jolly colt,

Like a weasel nice and thin,

Mouth as tasty as sloe gin—

Darting eyes and arching brows—

Playful as some baby cows!

Nicky to the kitchen sprang

And grabbed her by the sweet poon tang.

"Dear one, love me all at once,"

Quoth the handy Nicholas;

Alison wrenched herself away,

Then thought again, and said, "OK."

"That's filthy," Alison said.

"Thank you," I said.

And then—

Did you ever have a vague feeling that you were about to do something bad, which you would regret, and yet you did it anyway? Why does this happen?

I said to Alison, "You ought to write a poem about your brace."

She flinched, and then she blinked at me. "Why would I want to do that?" she said.

"Well I mean, making pancakes with your cousin is nice, but—you know. 'Early morning sunlight on the powdered pancake mix.' How far can you go with that? 'Egg white on her perfect hands.' Where's the pain? You can't tell me—"

But I saw she was crying, so I shut up.

"Let's go home," she said.

As I drove her back to her house something very strange happened. The crying got worse, and it became this kind of hiccupping thing that was awful; but then she took a lot of breaths and rubbed her face with her hands, and then it was as though she just squeezed the sadness out of herself, until it was gone. It was frightening! She looked up and turned to me and gave me a big smile—a real one, I'm sure, because it was the only kind Alison was capable of.

"Why are you smiling?" I said.

Twenty years, several towns, and two wives later, her response still has me puzzled.

"Because I don't want my parents to know you made me cry," she said.

When Jesus Lost His Head
by Karen Spears Zacharias

NEW ORLEANS—Jesus hasn't deserted the Ninth Ward. He stands statue-still on a lawn, around the corner from Jackson Barracks. His arms are open wide, ready to embrace any and all who are willing. But there's something terribly amiss with this Jesus.

The yard in which he stands is littered with the debris of what was once a neighborhood. A paring knife, the sort used to peel potatoes and apples, rests on the sidewalk. Blue jeans, a red shirt, and shiny tinsel hang from a tree. A child's motor scooter is upended on a rooftop. What houses, stores, or churches remain are tilted up on corners, broken in the middle, or bent over double like an aging man on a walker.

And this statue of Jesus has lost his head. It's gone. All of it. Somewhere in the chaos of Katrina, or its aftermath, Jesus was decapitated.

It's hard to put your trust in a Redeemer without

a head, or a city, or a country for that matter. Mucked-up thinking is too far-reaching. Months after the waters receded, President George W. Bush flew into New Orleans, stood on a street in the French Quarter, one of the least damaged areas of the city, and declared that the city was up and running, ready to embrace tourists.

Try telling that to the folks working at Mother's, one of New Orleans's most popular lunch counters. A bone-weary cashier grimaces as an impatient customer complains about the service. The cashier explains that the shorthanded staff is working twelve-hour shifts, six days a week. "We can't get nobody else to work," she says, "'cause nobody can find a place to live."

The folks at Jackson Barracks understand. They, too, are operating with a skeleton crew, down from two hundred to a dozen or so. Power is out to all but one of the Barracks's hundred-year-old structures.

When Katrina struck, approximately 3,500 Louisiana Guard troops were stationed in Iraq and Afghanistan. First Lieutenant Scott Lejeune was one of the members stationed in Baghdad. "I watched the hurricane on CNN, but you can't comprehend the magnitude of the devastation until you see it yourself. It's worse than anything I saw in Iraq," Lejeune said.

Forget all the images from television, in the newspapers, online. Not a one of them that truly captures what's left. Instead, walk out your front door, look around, and imagine for as far as you can see every house, every store, every church, every streetlight, every lawn ornament, every car, truck, SUV, or boat blasted to smithereens. Imagine the bombing of Berlin come to your neighborhood. Imagine Hiroshima. Imagine the end of the world. Then, and only then, can you really begin to understand what the folks driving into Jackson Barracks see every single day.

There are no dogs barking. No motors humming. No kids laughing. No horns blaring. No water running. No music of any sort. Graveyards aren't this quiet.

Lieutenant Colonel Casey Levy leans on a balcony railing and looks out across the Mississippi River and recalls the unworldly silence that fell over New Orleans after the levees broke.

"Each evening we watched as that dreaded darkness fell over the city," he said. "All we could hear was pitiful wailing from people trapped on their rooftops and the baleful howling of animals."

There was also the smell of a forty-foot, formerly

refrigerated trailer from a sausage factory down the street. It floated over the chain-link fence and landed right in front of the guardhouse. It remained there for the next month, full of rotting, rancid meat.

It's enough to turn a meat-and-potatoes man into a vegan. Even now, a musty smell lingers over the city. It's not the sort of mildewy smell one encounters in the beach houses along a rainy coastline. But rather the sort that occurs after you've discovered Aunt Pearlie dead in her bed, and realize that her twelve cats have had the run of the joint for the entire month of July.

"I'll never forget those smells," Levy said.

Four months before Katrina's wrath, a major told me of her concerns about the levees bursting. With so many troops overseas, she wasn't sure the Guard would have the manpower to handle it. At the time, I thought her comments were the ramblings of a mother-soldier worried about being shipped off to war. In hindsight, her worries seem almost prophetic.

One hundred high-water vehicles were brought into the Barracks the day before Katrina struck. A day later, when the Industrial Canal levee crumbled, as floodwaters rushed down St. Claude Avenue, "We knew something was happening," Levy said. "You could hear the roof on this building. It sounded as if it was breathing."

Then, as the old children's hymn says, *The rains came down and the floods came up,* and sent the staff scrambling for higher ground. In less than an hour Jackson Barracks was under ten to eleven feet of water. "We looked like ants running up the stair-wells," Levy said.

Over the next twenty-four hours those stairwells were designated "Him" and "Her" bathrooms. "You get used to the lowest level of human conditions imaginable real quickly when you're in that kind of situation," Levy added.

Communications systems were down. Vehicles couldn't move. "We were back to Pony Express," one officer said. "We had to rely on horse and pony."

Or boat and bike. Colonel Levy rescued a bike from the floodwaters, put it in a flat-bottomed boat, floated across the parade field and through the bar-racks's wrought-iron gates. When he reached a levee, he hopped on the bike, delivering messages to National Guard helicopters dropping supplies.

Helplessness joined the waters washing over Jackson Barracks. National Guard folks are trained to protect and aid their community. Levy and others like him, New Orleans natives, couldn't even check on their own families.

"I was stuck out here in Tombstone," Levy said, "unable to help or talk to my own family for almost three weeks."

Levy knows there are people even now who question why there wasn't a quicker response on the Guard's behalf. People sitting in the comfort of their homes in Seattle, Atlanta, or St. Paul who only had a camera-lens view of what was happening and who was handling it.

The citizen soldiers at Jackson Barracks were on the scene before and during the storm and remain there long after. New Orleans is their home—its citizens, their neighbors, their kin. Over fifty thousand National Guard members, from states throughout the nation, have worked on hurricane recovery. Every single one of those citizen soldiers volunteered for that duty.

"This is our Iraq," Levy said.

Driving down St. Claude Avenue, through the Ninth Ward, Levy fears that his beloved city will never be restored: "I can't explain what it's like," he said, "watching your city die."

Even more difficult to explain is why our nation's

leaders are so willing to allow that to happen. It appears that Jesus isn't the only public figure to have lost his head in the wake of a national disaster.

About the Contributors

Howard Bahr is a native of Mississippi.

Stuart Bloodworth teaches English at Motlow State Community College in Lynchburg, Tennessee. His poems have appeared in various journals, including *The North American Review, The Laurel Review, National Poetry Review, North Dakota Quarterly,* and *Poem.* He lives in Tullahoma, Tennessee, with his wife, Amy, and son, Jonathan.

Rick Bragg is the author of three best-selling books, including the critically acclaimed *All Over but the Shoutin'* and *Ava's Man,* both books that have become anthems for working-class people, and lasting love stories about the South. He is also the author of the best-selling *I Am a Soldier, Too,* and *Somebody Told Me.* Now Professor of Writing at the University of Alabama, he is a Harvard Nieman Fellow, winner of the Pulitzer Prize, and a two-time winner of the prestigious National Society of Newspaper Editors Distinguished Writing Award, as well as more than 50 other book and journalism awards. His next book, a story of his father, is expected out in the spring of 2007. His first novel is due out two years after that.

PIA Z. EHRHARDT lives in New Orleans, again, with her husband and son. Her stories have appeared in *McSweeney's, Mississippi Review, Quick Fiction,* and *Narrative Magazine.* She is the recipient of the 2005 Narrative Magazine Prize for Fiction. Her debut short story collection, *Famous Fathers*, and her novel, *Speeding in the Driveway,* will be published by MacAdam/Cage.

TOM FRANKLIN is the author of *Poachers*, a collection of stories, and the novels *Hell at the Breech* and *Smonk,* all published by William Morrow. A recipient of a 2001 Guggenheim Fellowship, Franklin lives in Oxford, Mississippi, and teaches at Ole Miss. He is married to the poet Beth Ann Fennelly.

WILLIAM GAY is the author of the novels *Provinces of Night* and *The Long Home,* as well as the short story collection *I Hate to See That Evening Sun Go Down.* He is the winner of the 1999 William Peden Award and the 1999 James Michener Memorial Prize and a recipient of a 2002 Guggenheim fellowship. His novel *Twilight* will be published by MacAdam/Cage this fall. He lives in Hohenwald, Tennessee.

L. A. HOFFER is a Ph.D. candidate in creative writing at the University of Tennessee, currently completing a novel about the twin towns of Bristol, Tennessee, and Bristol, Virginia. "Push" is one of a series of linked short stories set in Beech Mountain, North Carolina, the first of which appeared in *Blue Mesa Review.*

FRANK TURNER HOLLON is the author of five published novels, *The Pains of April, The God File, A Thin Difference, Life Is a Strange Place,* and *The Point of Fracture,* as well as a children's book, *Glitter Girl and the Crazy Cheese.* His short stories have appeared in *Stories from the Blue Moon Café,* Volumes I and II, and *The Alumni Grill.*

CHIP LIVINGSTON's poetry and fiction have appeared most recently in *Barrow Street, Bloom, McSweeney's, Mudfish, New York Quarterly, Ploughshares, Poetry Southeast,* and *Best New Poets 2005.* He lives in New York City.

THOMAS McGUANE has published numerous books of fiction and nonfiction, written three major motion pictures, and directed one. He was the Wallace Stegner Fellow in writing at Stanford University and received the Rosenthal Award from the American Academy of Arts and Letters. His work has been collected in *Best American Essays, Best American Sports Writing,* and *Best American Stories.* His latest book, *Gallatin Canyon,* will be published by Knopf in July.

JACK PENDARVIS is a contributor to the magazines *The Believer, The Oxford American, McSweeney's,* and *Paste.* He is the author of two books, *The Mysterious Secret of the Valuable Treasure* and the forthcoming *Your Body Is Changing.* He lives in Atlanta.

RON RASH is the author of three collections of poetry, two collections of stories, and three novels, the most recent of which is *The World Made Straight* (Henry Holt, 2006). He teaches at Western Carolina University. In 2005 he received the James Still Award from the Fellowship of Southern Writers.

JAMES WHORTON JR. is from Hattiesburg, Mississippi. He is author of the novels *Approximately Heaven* and *Frankland,* and his other work has appeared in *The Oxford American, Sewanee Review, Mississippi Review,* and *The Washington Post*. He teaches writing at SUNY Brockport.

KAREN SPEARS ZACHARIAS's commentary has been featured on National Public Radio and in the *New York Times*. She is the author of *After the Flag Has Been Folded* (William Morrow, 2006) and *Benched* (Mercer University Press, 1997). Karen is married to a pretty decent Yankee, and divides her time between her home in Oregon and her hometown in Georgia. She is working on a novel set in East Tennessee.